Death Makes A Move

A Taylor Texas Mystery

Vikki Walton

Death Makes A Move

For permission requests, write to the publisher:
Attention: Permissions Coordinator

Morewellson, Ltd.
P. O. Box 49726
Colorado Springs, Colorado 80949-9726

ISBN: 978-1- 950452-17-0 (standard edition print)
978-1-950452-16-3 (e-pub)
978-1-950452-18-7 (large print edition)

Front cover illustration: Mariah Sinclair
Publishing/design services: Wild seas formatting
Editing: Top Shelf editing services

Chapter One

The last box coming off the truck made everything final in Christie's mind. It still felt odd that she'd returned to the home she'd grown up after all these years away only to find the old homestead felt familiar, yet unknown at the same time. After her father's fall caused her concern for his on-going welfare and safety, coupled with the constant harassment of developers after him to sell their property, Christie had made the difficult decision to return home for good. She'd spent the last few months packing up her life as she knew it and had ended her contract with the hospice facility. She hoped that her return to Comfort, Texas would be a good decision on her part.

Pop opened the door and stuck his head out. "How much more do you like?"

"This is it, Pop." Christie transferred the box to her other hip as it grew heavy. The rest of her furniture and items were in storage until she resolved her housing situation. She'd been diligent in putting money away in savings for many years as she tended to live frugally, so she didn't need to look for work, at least until the coming year. That would give her time to get settled and decide if she wanted to work in San Antonio, Kerrville, or possibly Boerne, if a situation became available. She'd thought of starting her own traveling hospice service, but maybe it was time to move into something that brought her more joy. While she knew the care, she provided her patients was important, she wanted to focus on life instead of death for a change.

Christie shifted the box from her hip into her arms and trudged toward the house. Mutt and Jeffrey, their tails wagging excitedly, danced around her feet. She loved the happiness the two labs exhibited but it was making it difficult to move more than a few paces at a time. "You guys. I love you too, but please, move out of the way."

After Pop called them with a whistle, the dogs lay down on the porch. He held the door open for Christie who set the box next to the other few boxes in the small living room. "Moving is a lot harder in my forties than it was in my twenties." She rubbed the small of her back. "Glad that's the last of the boxes."

"Pfft. Wait until you hit your seventies, then we'll talk, girly." Pop grinned.

Christie walked through to the back bedroom and sat the box down on the bed. She glanced at another stack of boxes containing her mother's items. "We ready?"

Pop sighed and shook his head. "Ready."

Christie strode over to the boxes and bags marked with tape reading, "Pass it On." Before she'd left Comfort on her last visit, she and Pop had gone through her mother's clothing and sewing items, gathering up what they could give away or items they could recycle in other ways. But they hadn't had time to finish and Pop had said he'd handle the rest. Now what was left of her mother's things had been whittled down to a few boxes and bags. Tears sprung to her eyes and she wiped them away. "I still miss her. Even after all these years."

"Me too, hon." Pop squeezed her shoulder.

Christie grabbed a couple of bags, and her father

did the same. They headed out to her new blue Chevy truck. She'd tricked it out with an automatic step, side wheel storage, easy access to the bed with steps, and other features that would come in handy, now that she would be helping on Pop's ranch. She'd hated to part with her old Jeep, but she needed a vehicle she could depend on now that it would see more use.

After they'd dropped off the clothing and other items, Christie remarked, "How about grabbing some mijas at High's?"

"I don't know. I hate to spend money going out."

"Pop, it's my money. I'm paying."

"Yep, but I have to think about you and now, Jess, coming to stay."

When Christie had mentioned the idea of the teenager coming to live with them, she'd expected strong pushback against it, but her father had been surprisingly willing to take Jess in to stay with them. The help Jess could provide around the ranch could turn into a real blessing for her father when she was busy at work. The reason Jess had to live with them saddened her, but she couldn't control the actions of others. This was one way to speak into a young life and help them through a tough time.

"Pop, you know we're not here for you to take care of us. I have my own money, and Mike has already given me the breakdown on how he will provide for Jess while he's in school."

After some more cajoling, the pair enjoyed mijas and coffee, before returning home to the ranch. A mailing tube poked out of the large parcel box next to the mailbox and newspaper slot.

"Oh, that must be my blueprints! Perfect timing." Christie exited the truck and examined the address.

"I don't understand why you want to live in a spaceship. Makes no sense to me." Pop shook his head.

"It's not a spaceship, Pop. It's an earthship."

"What I said. Some kind of weird thing. Why not just build a regular home?"

"I had thought about getting a tiny home—"

"You mean a trailer?"

"Well, I guess, realistically, that's what they are, but if I will live here, I want to have something that works with the land. Now that I took that permaculture class and toured some homes, I like the idea of it."

"I don't know." He removed his old, tatty Stetson, wiped his brow and then placed the felt hat back on his head.

"Actually, don't worry about it, Pop. I'm fairly certain I'm not going to build an earthship because of building regulations and restrictions. This plan is for a cordwood house the architect recommended when we discussed other possibilities. You've been saying for years that you want to clear out a bunch of the cedar trees on the property. This is a way to use that wood for a good purpose at the same time. I thought, well, you might want to help with building the house."

"I don't know. I'll have to check my calendar." He winked at her.

Christie smiled. "I figure if we can cut the wood early this fall, we'll be ready next spring."

Her father's phone rang. She heard him say, "Curtis" as he answered. "Um. Uh, huh. Yep."

Laughing, Christie said, "You're so eloquent with your words."

“They get the job done. That’s all that’s needed in my book.”

“So how is Curtis?” Christie shivered as she remembered finding Curtis Altgelt badly hurt on her last visit home. He’d been discovered almost unconscious with a nasty hit to his head next to the fence line that adjoined their ranches. If they hadn’t found him, he could have died. With no one to help him at home, Curtis had gone to a long-term care facility until he could manage on his own.

“He’s being discharged and wanted to know if we’d come pick him up.”

Christie pushed the gate-opener and waited as it swung open. They’d never needed a gate before, but with anyone able to access the property, Christie had convinced her father to get one. “Of course. I’m sure he’ll be happy to be back in his own bed at home.”

She drove the truck through and hit the button to close the gate.

Pop’s eyes narrowed. “True that. Plus, the vultures have been circling even closer.”

“Which ones?” Christie and her father had had a

run-in with Curtis's stepsons, who were determined to make millions off of the Altgelt ranch. They were also dealing with the Websters—Emma and Tyler, developers intent on getting the Altgelt ranch and the Taylor property. At least they'd quit showing up at the property unannounced since Pop installed the gate. Only those they knew and trusted had the entry code.

"The boys are still trying to work around him, saying he's not mentally competent to handle his property."

"Oh, that makes me so angry. Curtis is still as sharp as a tack. The last time I visited with him, we played cards and chatted. His short-term memory is fine, and trust me, I've dealt with a lot of Alzheimer's and dementia patients. Curtis has no such problem."

"Tell that to Curtis. He still wonders about it."

"Has he been having anymore issues since he moved into the care facility?"

"Only once or twice. But you have to wonder..."

"About?"

"Those were also the times when the boys came to visit him. They left before he got to see them. He was often in physical therapy when they visited, but Curtis swears his room looked different when he got back."

"That's convenient for them. They can say they visited but not really have to speak with him. Plus that could have given them ample time in his room alone. Do you think they were looking for anything?"

"Probably. I bet they're foaming at the mouth, trying to see what his will says and where it is. But Curtis is too smart to let them get their hands on it. I have a copy at the house in my safe, and he also put one in a safe deposit box at the bank."

"That's good. I know he wants to honor his promise to his wife, but I wouldn't give that scum a blade of grass from that land."

"Don't worry your pretty head there, now, girly. It's all taken care of. They will get land, and Curtis will do right by Marilyn."

"I'm not sure about Curtis staying by himself, though."

Pop replied, "Agreed. But he won't be having no help. I plan to spend time with him. Maybe you could bring us a pie."

Christie laughed. "Is this for Curtis or you?"

"Well..." He stroked his chin as if thinking about her statement.

She rolled her eyes at his display. "Fine. What kind? Pumpkin? Apple?"

"Yum. Both sound good, but I was thinking Ranch Pot Pie."

Christie walked toward the kitchen and peered into the fridge. "Looks like you have most of the ingredients here. I can do that, too. Dessert?"

Pop had followed her into the kitchen and pulled out a basket of potatoes. "Caramel apple pie sounds mighty good right about now."

"You have any Granny Smith apples on hand, or do I need to go to Lowe's Market for some?"

"I believe there's some in the root cellar you can use. If not, I can go into town and get some."

They had some time before picking up Curtis, so Christie set to work on making piecrust she could use in the pies later. After she'd finished making the dough and putting it in the fridge, she spent a while on getting her items unpacked in the bedroom. Time flew by, and they were soon setting off down IH10 into San Antonio to the care facility to retrieve Curtis.

They arrived to find him sitting in the dayroom. "Bout Time. A fella needs his own space." He motioned at the nurse. "Come on, missy. Daylight's-a-wasting."

The nurse and Christie exchanged a knowing smile, reflecting their shared experience in dealing with cantankerous patients.

After they'd loaded Curtis in the truck, a silence descended on the vehicle, each lost in their own thoughts.

Finally, Curtis spoke. "I wanted to say thank you for coming to get me. Seems like them boys are stirring up more trouble. They're taking me to court."

"What? Hey!" Christie laid on her horn. "Sorry, what do you mean they're taking you to court?"

"They came by yesterday and said if I didn't let them see my will, they would take me to court."

"For what?" Christie shot him a curious glance. "They don't have any right to see your will unless you want them to." She'd met some greedy people during her time working with patients, but this had to top them all.

"They think I'm an old fool who doesn't know up from down. I sure wish I would have tarred their hides when they were younger. Maybe that would have knocked some sense into them."

"Well, we need to think about this. How about we figure it out over some Ranch Pot Pie?"

"Now that's the way to my heart. Christie, you could win any man over with your cooking. You know, time has a way of creeping up on you."

Christie chose not to respond. In her twenties, like many women, she'd considered getting married and having children, but she had been so independent, years ticked by. Now that she had reached her forties, she didn't know if that would be something that she'd consider. Plus, she didn't see any man fawning over a forty-something woman who lived with her father and who would be caring for a teenage boy.

Taking the Comfort exit, they drove until they reached the turnoff for the Curtis spread. The truck easily took the larger potholes, and the new shocks kept Curtis and her father comfortable with the ride.

Curtis's place could use with some road maintenance, too. They rounded the bend and spied two vehicles in front of the old homestead—a silver Mercedes and a white company truck Christie and her father had become far too familiar with in the last months.

"Hot da—" the words exploded out of Curtis. "It's like they're dancing on my grave. Gimme your shotgun, R.C."

Christie sighed. "Curtis, Pop doesn't carry a shotgun in *my* truck. Or his, for that matter."

Curtis gave a disgusted sigh. "These new-fangled days."

Christie pulled up next to the truck. Tyler Webster stood up from his position of leaning against the vehicle. Sunglasses hid the men's eyes, but as soon as they spotted R.C., the two brothers jolted and stepped back. Christie laughed at how Pop had brought Erik to his knees for his insolence on their last visit. Nick had been smart enough to stay silent.

Pop and Curtis exited the truck and Christie went around the front to join them.

"Mr. Altgelt." Tyler Webster extended his hand.

"I don't recall inviting you out here." Curtis ignored Tyler's outstretched hand and propped himself against the truck.

"Erik called me. They wanted me to give them an idea about future development potential. They want to ensure that you have the best care for retirement—"

"Hogwash. They want to know how much they stand to make when I kick off."

"Mr. Altgelt, I know that we haven't been able to speak before, but I can assure you, we provide the best commission for our clients, and I can easily state that we will get you a fair price—"

"Listen, young fella." Curtis pointed an arthritic finger at Tyler. "I don't want you to go wasting your breath like all the others. I ain't selling. Now. Or ever."

"But—" Tyler pushed back the fringe that had fallen toward his eyes.

"But nothing. No sale. Leave." He pointed to Erik and Nick who had remained quiet during the exchange. "Your mama would be nothing short but ashamed of you boys. Glad she's not here for you to break her heart." He shook his head in disgust. "You can follow this here fella out of here." He pointed to Tyler, then motioned to Pop. "Come on R.C., something smells bad out here."

When the two elderly men entered the house, Tyler, Nick, and Erik faced Christie. She shrugged and grinned.

"Do you think this is funny?" Erik took a step forward. "I'm still thinking of pressing assault charges against your old man."

Christie recalled her father easily subduing Erik with a simple acupressure technique after he'd threatened them. "Go ahead. I'd love for you to explain how you screamed like a little girl while my dad gripped your hand."

"Make jokes. But I'm deadly serious." Erik flinched as Nick grabbed his arm to stop him.

Her voice lowered, and she took a step toward him, causing him to step back. "I'm serious, too. Don't you *ever* threaten my father...or me."

"Or?"

"Or you'll be sorry." She stared at him, knowing she'd won many such contests with her patients' relatives.

Tyler Webster laughed and waved his arms. "Let's stop the OK Corral stuff. It's unfortunate, but at some point, Mr. Altgelt will be unable to care for himself or pass away. Then, Erik and Nick each have a legal right to this property as heirs. We're just trying to look at the possibilities. This will help Mr. Altgelt too." He laid his hand on Erik's forearm as a silent signal to stop, "No harm, no foul, right?"

Erik shrugged off Tyler's hand but nodded consent.

Christie answered Tyler while keeping Erik in her peripherals. "The only possibilities you're trying to look at are how much you stand to make off the hard work of an old man and the generations before him." Christie bristled. "People are living to ripe old ages now. Some are living past one hundred years old."

Erik whispered, "Not if I can help it."

Chapter Two

After leaving them, Christie made a list of errands and set off to Boerne. She turned off the podcast about living with teens so she could think. Erik's words echoed in Christie's mind. Had he been joking, or as he'd said, was he being deadly serious? Could Erik or Nick have been behind the things going on at Curtis's house? First there had been a barn fire before Christie had visited. Had they caused that? Curtis had almost died from an accident and Christie being home at the time had most likely saved his life. Had someone piled the stand of rocks exactly where Curtis would fall if his foot fell into the dug hole?

Curtis had struggled after the accident, and even though he hadn't complained, Christie could see that the fall he'd taken had left him with more aches and pains than before. If Erik or Nick had caused it, she would make them pay for what they'd done.

But something else had been nagging at Christie.

After Webster employee, Hector Garcia had been tragically killed on their property, had another death occurred because of something she'd said in passing to his killer? If so, she needed to tell the woman's family about it. She had to make amends, if need be, and let the family know that the woman's death wasn't simply due to old age.

Driving into Boerne, Christie pulled up to the curb and looked at the house across the street from where Hector had lived. The door which used to be pink had now been painted a vivid magenta. She hoped whoever lived there now could give her some information on the last owner.

Bracing herself, she knocked on the door. She waited. Another knock. A curtain moved. Christie waved. It dropped back into place, and the door opened.

"It's you!" Christie exclaimed.

The woman's puzzled expression transformed to mirth as her face lit up. "Yes. It's you, too, dearie. Can I help you?"

Christie blurt out. "But I thought—I guess I was

wrong ..."

The women smiled up at Christie. "Why don't you come in, and you can tell me all about it over a cup of tea."

Christie followed the woman inside. The unusual paint color choice on the door should have indicated the interior would also be unique on the inside, but Christie's stunned expression must have been evident on her face.

"What do you think?" The woman swept her hand out to showcase the room.

She'd decorated the room in a unique style of "modern meets Victorian" with a splash of the "roaring twenties" thrown in. The woman beamed as Christie's gaze found new delights everywhere she looked.

"I—" Christie began.

"I can see that you're at a loss for words. I always loved certain styles, and once my dear Marcus passed away, I thought, I'm not getting any younger. So why not surround myself with things that make me happy and make me smile?"

"I agree," nodded Christie. "I think we often spend

too much time trying to fit in and not enough time being true to ourselves."

"Honey, I never try to fit in." The woman's eyes sparkled with merriment.

Her statement was evident from her green polka dot pants, a yellow and red striped blouse, a variety of multi-colored bracelets, and a necklace and earrings in green, red, yellow, and white. The costume jewelry she wore appeared to be from around the forties and if the pieces were original Bakelite was highly prized and valuable. Now that Christie could see the woman up close, she noted that the woman's gray hair was buzzed short against her scalp. Her unlined face belied her years which was free of makeup, save a slick of lip gloss. Her hazel eyes sparkled, and what was most likely veneers gave the impression of youth. The woman could have been sixty or ninety.

"Follow me." The woman walked into a hallway and motioned for Christie to follow. Looking back at the front room, Christie smiled.

That room makes me happy.

The spry woman's bracelets jangled as she made

her way into what was a newer part of the home. From the house facade, Christie would never have guessed that such an extension existed. Here, an open plan held a kitchen, dining area, and living room. While the front room had been quirky, in this section of the house, the furnishings were more subdued with bright white walls. But that's not what captured Christie's attention.

"Whoa." Everywhere she turned, art drew her in. Sculptures, paintings, metalwork, and along one wall was the most beautiful hanging she'd ever seen. "This is stunning!"

"Thank you. I think it's one of my best so far."

"You did this!"

"Yes," the woman replied humbly. "I was inspired by the artist, Eta Ingham Lawrie. I saw her work when I visited Alnwick in the UK and it led to me trying my hand at weaving. If you want to see some stunning work, check out her weaving. It's beautiful."

She stood next to Christie. "Would you like to see my loom?"

"Yes."

"Okay, I'll be happy to show you. But I think we should start with introductions first." She thrust out her hand. "I'm Orchid Merryweather."

"Christie. Christie Taylor." They shook hands. "Nice to meet you."

"Let me put the kettle on and you can tell me all about how I surprised you." She made her way to the kitchen area while Christie followed behind her.

"I have to say; that's a unique name."

"My mama loved flowers. When she was first married, she couldn't have a big garden, so she named her girls after flowers." She ticked off her fingers each sporting a decorative ring. "Rose, Daisy, Peony, Tulip...glad I didn't get Chrysanthemum. Not surprisingly, she goes by her middle name."

"Wow. That's a lot of children and all daughters."

"Oh, my mother had twelve children by the time it was all said and done."

Christie shook her head. "I can't even imagine caring for one, much less twelve."

Orchid removed the whistling teapot from the stove and poured the water into another container.

"When one of Daisy's kids got to be an adult, they asked, 'Nana, why did you have so many children?' My mother said, 'Well, I've always been hard of hearing. At night, Papa would say, 'do you want to go to bed or what?' I'd always reply, 'What?'"

Orchid winked at Christie, who burst out laughing.

Christie watched as Orchid went through the process of putting tea leaves into a tea ball. Christie felt the stress leaving her shoulders and her mind slowing down. When everything was ready, Orchid picked up a tray and had Christie open the back door. They walked through a gate covered in honeysuckle and into a large garden.

"This is beautiful." Christie turned to admire all the plants.

"I love it back here. It's a good place to come and commune with nature." Orchid set the tray down on a table that sat under a covering of grapevines. When they'd settled back on soft-cushioned chairs, Orchid took a deep breath, then spoke. "Now, Christie. I have a confession to make."

Christie raised her eyes to meet Orchid's.

"Sorry, but I didn't eat your pie. I just don't like rhubarb."

Laughter spilled from Christie's lips. "Well, it's a good thing because it probably saved your life!"

"What? Now you really must tell me." She rinsed out a pot with the hot water, then poured water into a strainer over tea leaves.

Christie briefly recapped what had happened with Hector, who had lived in the house across the street from Orchid. "So you see, Hector's killer thought that you were a witness and could point the finger at them. In order to make sure you wouldn't say anything, they tried to get rid of you by giving you a pie they said I'd made for you. Thankfully, it was one you don't like. But that pie could have proven fatal if you'd eaten it."

"Oh, my. Well, that young woman simply said you had baked me a pie. I still have the pie pan and carrier. I thought that was why you came."

"Can I see it?"

"Certainly. But let's get to know one another first." She handed Christie a cup of tea, a fragrant Darjeeling. Christie added a touch of cream while Orchid drank hers with a slice of lemon and one sugar cube. "I believe we are kindred spirits."

"Ahh, I love Anne of Green Gables."

"Me too. I think that is one of the best sayings about the connection that can be felt between two people, don't you agree?"

Christie nodded while sipping at her tea. After a bit of coaxing and feeling comfortable with Orchid, Christie shared stories about her life before moving back to Comfort. She also shared about what had happened on her vacation at the bed-and-breakfast in Colorado, which had precipitated her work sabbatical and return home. Finally, she spoke about how Hector's truck had barely missed her father, causing Pop to fall hard and break his shoulder. "So all that to say, I figured that I needed to come home." Christie accepted another cup of tea from Orchid.

After expressing her sadness at the earlier events, Orchid shared some of her life stories, like her march with Martin Luther King across the Edmund Pettus Bridge.

"Wow. It's like speaking to living history."

"I hope I'm not that old. I went with my parents and sisters. At the time I just recall being tired of walking so much. Of course, I understand the significance now." She poured more tea into her cup.

The pair laughed as the minutes ticked by.

Christie listened and then asked, "I hope I'm not getting to personal and you can tell me if it's not of my business. You never married?"

"Surprised? I know in my day, that was more expected, but I had too many things I wanted to see and do. I've spoiled my nieces and nephews, but it was the right choice for me. I don't see a ring on your finger. Same choice?"

Christie shrugged. "It just never really happened. Not sure if it will now."

"You never know what the Good Lord has in store for us. That's what makes each day so exciting!" Orchid gathered up the tea items and Christie offered to carry the tray inside.

"Let me get you that pan before I forget."

They strolled back toward the house. The large cat clock with moving eyes and tail let Christie know she had been there for hours. "Oh, wow. I didn't realize it has been that long. I hope I didn't take up your time from something else."

"Not at all. But you have given me an idea. If you don't mind, could you come back? I'll show you the weaving machine then. When creativity strikes, you need to catch it before it flies away."

"I'd love to. Do you have some paper? I can give you my phone number?"

Orchid pulled the latest phone from her pocket. "What's your number? I'll text you." The woman's fingers flew over the keys not unlike so many of the teenagers Christie spied. A beep on her own phone showed her the text had gone through. She smiled at seeing the long line of emojis. A flower. A tea pot. A calendar. A date. A time.

"Terrific." She held out her hand as Orchid gave her the pan and container. After saying their goodbyes, Christie headed to her truck. She unlocked her truck and sat the items on the front passenger seat. Moving around to the driver's side, Christie glanced over at the house across the street where Hector had lived. New cars sat in the driveway, and two young children played in the front yard as a young woman who appeared to be in her twenties watched over them. An older woman with her hair cut in a short auburn bob came out of the house carrying two glasses. After handing one to a child, she waved at Christie, who returned the wave.

Christie finished her errands and enjoyed the drive back home, but her feeling of contentment came crashing down as she spied not just one but two white trucks in front of the gate to her Pop's place.

Not the Websters again.

With them parked in front of her, she couldn't drive past them. She shoved the truck in park and prepared to do battle. Christie lowered her window.

Emma strode toward Christie purposefully. "Hello," she trilled.

Uh, oh.

"We heard you are moving back to the area."

"Yes."

"Well, I'm not sure if you know this, but we are also custom home builders, as well as developers. We thought we'd come out and give you our card and one of our brochures." Her sickly-sweet smile forced Christie to not roll her eyes. She glanced over at Tyler Webster, who stood next to his truck. His demeanor signaled a desire to leave so they must have been waiting for a while.

Christie stole a glance at the brochure offered by Emma. On the front, a typical rock and stucco styled house with a four-car garage held center place. "I appreciate your thinking of me but I'm looking at something smaller."

Emma smiled back. "I know you don't want to sell. I'm just saying that a few areas close to the Altgelt ranch would give you a nice sum for building your dream home and decorating it. Maybe even a bit left over for some fun." She winked at Christie like they were best friends.

"Again, we're not selling. As for my dream home, I plan to build a cordwood home."

"A what?" Emma quickly composed herself. "I'm sorry. I thought you said a 'cordwood' house." She laughed but it fell flat.

"That's exactly what I said. Cordwood homes are very sustainable and can last up to one hundred and fifty years. Plus, wood such as cedar has a good R-value making it energy efficient and is naturally decay resistant." She waved her hand toward the trees. "As you can see, we have tons of cedar on our property."

Emma's pleasant façade cracked, "I *know* what a cordwood house is. That's not what I meant. However, that—" She clamped her mouth shut when Tyler interrupted her by calling her name.

Christie looked from Emma to Tyler, then realized why Emma was so upset. Once they had developed the Altgelt land, they most likely wanted to expand the development toward Pop's land. They must have thought Christie would build one of those horrible, ridiculously large homes she despised. Because of the location of the property, it would be easy to see her new house, which she felt Emma would consider in poor taste. Plus, possibly drive prices down on the property the Websters wanted to develop.

Another smile from Emma. "Well, you have lots of property. Will you be building close to your father's place and tearing that down?"

"Why would we do that?"

Tyler had joined Emma and finally spoke. "Emma probably thought you would build something bigger for you and your father."

"Have you met my father?"

Christie and Tyler snorted, but Emma did not join in.

"Good point," Tyler responded.

"My father will live in that house the rest of his days, God willing. I'm building the other house for me."

"You know that quite a large area of your property is in the floodplain and building there would be waiting for disaster."

Christie pushed her hair back off her face and tucked it behind her ears. "I know. That's why I plan to build the property up on beams."

Where had that come from? That's not your plan.

"What?" Emma squealed as Tyler grabbed her wrist, but she jerked away.

"With the house up, I'll have great views, and it will

provide a covered lower space for entertaining." The more Christie thought about it, the more the idea sounded fantastic. This is something she should really consider. It probably wouldn't take much to change her plans for it.

BANG!

They all jumped at the sound of gunfire.

"Is that your father?" Tyler glanced around, searching intently with his eyes.

"No. It didn't come from the direction of the house. It came from over there." She pointed toward the back area of the property headed toward Curtis's spread.

Christie pulled out her phone and called her father. She wasted no time in sharing the reason for her call. "Pop, I heard gunshots. Do you know if anyone is out shooting today?" She listened and signed off. "Okay. Bye."

"Pop says he and Curtis have a deal where they let hunters come in and cull the deer and hogs. They give them a strong perimeter and a limited window. He thinks that window is open for the next three weeks. It's only in a designated area, so we're safe here."

Emma shivered with revulsion. Christie, seeing her reaction, added, “This is taking some getting used to for me too, as well. I may have grown up out here, but I’ve lived in the city for a long time. Hearing gunshots is definitely something I’m not accustomed to hearing, either.”

The trio turned as another of the Websters trucks drove toward them. It was Cole, once a high school flame of Christie’s, but now they were simply acquaintances. Another man in his fifties sat in the passenger seat. The pair exited the cab and joined them.

The man spoke to Christie, “Hi. I’m Kurt. Kurt Matthews.” He extended a hand, which Christie shook.

“Have we met before?” she responded. “You look so familiar.”

“Don’t think so. I just moved here with my family from Oklahoma after receiving a job offer from these fine people.” He pointed to the Websters.

Christie struggled not to tell him to run. She looked at him closer. He looked to be in his fifties with salt and pepper, thinning hair and a mustache. His face was freckled from the sun and age, but Christie could swear she'd met him before. Must be that crazy deja-vu thing. "You must remind me of someone, I guess."

"Well, you know what they say. We all have doppelgangers roaming around." He winked at her.

"Yes, that's true." She smiled back at him. "Anyway, nice to meet you. Are you living in Comfort?"

"No. We're renting a small place from Webster Realty until we find something larger. We have my daughter and the grandkids living with us, too, for now."

"Wait. The house in Boerne?"

He cocked his head. "Um, yep. Why?"

I saw them when I was visiting Orchid."

"Orchid?"

"She's your neighbor. Across the street."

"Ah, yes. We've met her. Um, nice lady."

Christie laughed. "A bit eccentric, though?"

"Your words; not mine," he quipped.

Cole interrupted them. "I'm taking him out to see the various properties for sale and those in the pipeline."

"As long as you're not including our property or the Altgelt ranch in that tour."

Cole bristled but didn't respond.

Christie folded her arms over her chest. Whatever attraction she'd had for Cole in high school had been replaced with a general dislike.

Cole glanced at the Websters and Tyler chimed in. "Actually, they have an appointment with Mr. Altgelt. He wants to get an idea of the value of the property."

Her mind raced, but Christie said nothing as the pair climbed back into the truck and drove off. She needed to get with Pop and find out what was going on with Curtis. Had he changed his mind now that he'd been home for a while? She hoped not, but it wasn't her decision to make. However, the thought of a bunch of new homes next to her property sent shivers up her spine.

After Cole and Kurt drove off, Emma and Tyler followed suit. Christie was glad to see their taillights in her rearview mirror before opening the gate.

Chapter Three

Back home, she called Pop to let him know it may be later before she could get the pies over to them. She hadn't expected to spend so much time with Orchid but had enjoyed visiting with the lady. Christie let Pop know that if they wanted to eat sooner, she could make the pies for lunch tomorrow. However, Pop said they'd eat a snack before dinner if needed.

Having worked with the elderly, Christie knew that their appetites often took a nosedive, so she doubted they'd eat anything before she brought the pies. She quickly set to work making the ranch pie. She remembered how her mother had often made stew and used the leftovers in a pie. Over the years, many had requested the savory pie far more than the stew, and the pie had become an easy way to make a filling, hearty meal. She decided to make work on the caramel apple pie first.

~~~~~~~~~~
~~~~~~~~~~

Caramel Pie Recipe

Caramel

Ingredients and Amounts

- Butter (room temperature) 1 cup plus extra if needed for buttering pan
- Brown Sugar 1 pound
- Sweetened Condensed Milk 1 14 ounce can
- Light Corn Syrup 1 8 ounce cup
- Sea Salt (pinch) plus extra coarse sale if desired for salted caramel
- Vanilla 2 teaspoons

Items Needed On Hand:

- Measuring Cups and Spoons
- Heavy-bottom Medium Size Pot
- Wooden spoon with long handle or silicone heat-resistant spatula
- Candy thermometer
- Metal spoon (for checking hardness of candy)
- Baking pan (9x13)
- Kitchen shears/scissors
- *Optional: Silicone Mat*

Prepare your baking pan by either buttering the pan or placing a silicone mat inside on the bottom of the pan.

Combine all items in a heavy-bottom medium pot. Cook over medium heat until mixture comes to a boil.

Cook, stirring constantly until thermometer reaches 240 degrees (116 degrees C). If you do not have a thermometer, you can test by dropping a tiny amount into a spoon or container with cold water. The mixture should form a soft ball that flattens when removed from water.

Carefully pour the hot mixture into the baking pan. If salted caramel is desired, sprinkle a bit of coarse sea salt over the top as desired. Allow the mixture to cool to where it is flexible still but not hard. Don't allow it to fully cool so it can be cut. Using clean, sharp kitchen shears, cut the caramel into long thin strips approximately one-half inch in size. Scoring with a knife or the scissors first may help with this.

When complete, cut to size of pie pan. Any leftover pieces, twist into decorative caramels. Set the caramel ribbons aside.

Apple Pie Filling

Ingredients and Amounts

- Granny Smith Apples or tart, firm apples 4 cups, cubed or if preferred, thinly sliced.
- Organic Lemon
- Water 3 cups. Reserve one cup to mix the

flour/cornstarch to thicken the sauce.
- Brown Sugar ½ cup (in a pinch you can use white sugar and add a bit of molasses).
- White Sugar ½ cup
- Flour 1/3 cup (can also use cornstarch)
- Cinnamon ½ teaspoon
- Nutmeg (pinch)
- Sea Salt (pinch)

Items Needed On Hand:

- Measuring Cups and Spoons
- Heavy-bottom Medium Size Pot
- Wooden spoon with long handle or silicone heat-resistant spatula
- Whisk
- Kitchen shears
- Zester

Peel and core the apples. Cut into desired size. Wash and zest the outside of the washed lemon and use the juice and zest to coat the cut apples which prevents browning and gives a nice tang in contrast to the sweet of the pie filling and caramel.

Pour two cups of water into pot and combine the sugar, cinnamon, nutmeg and salt. With the remaining cup, combine the thickening agent of flour or cornstarch and whisk to remove any clumps. Add slowly to combined ingredients in pot, whisking into the ingredients to remove any formed clumps. Bring ingredients to boiling point, stirring until thickened. Add apples to mixture and coat evenly. Bring heat down to simmer until apples are still firm but softened.

Preparing the Pie

Heat oven to 400 degrees (204.4 C).

Items Needed On Hand:

Pie Crust

- Pie Crust (bottom and top required)
- Egg (optional)
- Coarse Sugar (optional)
- Coarse Salt (optional)

In prepared pie crust, add the apple mixture. Using the prepared caramel, lay one strip top to bottom and one strip in the middle side to side. If the strips are too long, clip with kitchen shears and save to eat or decorate top of pie. If done earlier, you can twist these same pieces and add to the pie top when cool. Repeat in open spaces around the pie until you have the desired amount of caramel you want for the pie. At a minimum, you will want at least one to two strips of caramel per pie slice.

For Pie Top

Top the pie with the crust and crimp edges to form seal. Using a fork or knife, cut an opening for steam to escape.

Optional:

Brush the top with egg wash.

Sprinkle coarse sugar over top or combination of coarse sugar and salt.

Bake the pie for 50 minutes. Check and if the crust is done, cover with foil or a pie crust protector for duration of cooking time so the crust doesn't burn.

Cool before cutting.

Serve with ice cream, whipped cream, or sliced cheddar.

Enjoy!

~~~~~~~~~~

As the fragrant apple and cinnamon smell filled the air, Christie worked on the Ranch Pie. After peeling the russet potatoes, Christie chopped up yellow onion and garlic before sautéing them in butter. She'd already
~~~~~~~~~~

cooked a chuck roast for carne guisada, so she'd taken some of the tenderized seasoned beef to add to the ranch pie. That would save some time in preparing the dish. Adding diced carrots and potatoes, along with the onion and garlic mixture, Christie combined the ingredients with mushroom soup and beef broth to coat everything. Finally she added the cooked beef. As Christie scooped the mixture into a pie shell, she kept going back to meeting Kurt. He certainly looked familiar. Maybe she'd seen him on the road or getting groceries at HEB at some point.

She smoothed down the mixture evenly and affixed the top crust to the pie. As soon as the caramel apple pie was done, she popped the Ranch Pie in the oven. Savory smells filled the air and her stomach rumbled. "Looks like I'm the one who needs a snack." Christie poked her head in the fridge and decided to make a salad to go with the Ranch Pie. She snacked on carrots as she added items to the fresh salad.

~~~

After loading up the pies, Christie headed over to
~~~

the Altgelt ranch for dinner. Arriving at the house, she flinched after hearing another gunshot.

I hope that this will be over soon. Not sure I can deal with much more of this.

She reached in and grabbed the ranch pie; the still warm container required a dishtowel to hold. Christie handed it to Pop, who she'd called before leaving to let him know she was on her way. He had come around to her side of the truck and she handed him the meat pie. She then took hold of the caramel apple pie, still warm from the oven. The cinnamon and apple mixture made her mouth water. With her free hand, she reached in and grabbed a bag that contained all the salad fixings to go with the meat pie. Christie pulled back from the truck and nudged the door shut with her hip.

"Howdy!" Curtis had appeared from around the house, a rifle lowered by his side. "Need help?"

"Nope. Got it. Thanks." She waved him ahead, and he took the gun into another room. "I'll clean it later," he said upon returning to the kitchen, where Christie was pulling romaine lettuce, and avocado from the bag.

"Oh, shoot. Forgot the tomatoes." She wiped her hands on her jeans.

"No worries. I have some out in the back. I had to go out there and chase off more of those pesky Grackles. They're becoming a dang nuisance. Getting into my crops; just all kinds of mischief."

"Is that what you were doing with the gun?"

"Yep." Pulling out an old, red handkerchief, he wiped his face and neck with it before stuffing it back in his pocket. "I sometimes go out and shoot into the trees, so they don't make nests there. My corn's coming up, and I don't want them thinking this is a great spot to put down roots."

"How about putting up a scarecrow?"

"Not had much luck with that, but I guess it wouldn't hurt none to try it."

Christie went to the sink and washed her hands. "Do you have any old clothes? We can make one up tomorrow. I can help you with it."

Curtis patted Christie on the hand. "I can see why ol' R.C. is so happy to have you home. I have missed you, girl."

"Thanks, Curtis. But to be honest, I'm tired of hearing the gunshots."

"Ah, you've turned into a city girl, have ya? Well, this isn't normal. The birds are bad this year and we have an abundance of critters that get up to all kinds of mischief."

"I have no right to say what you do; I just know I'm not keen on it. That's all."

"Understood. Again, glad you're back home. Especially," he rubbed his hands, "now that you're bringing me such good home cooking."

Christie chuckled, "Ah, so now I see why you're really happy I'm here." She washed and tore up the lettuce while Pop followed Curtis out to grab some tomatoes. By the time they'd returned, Christie had set the table, and she cut the ranch pie into serving sizes. "That took a while. I thought you all were hungry."

At the sink, Curtis soaped his hands and handed the bar to Pop. "We got to talking."

"About?" Christie sat at the end close to the stove. "Anything you want to share?"

Curtis sat at the head of the table and bowed his

head. After a prayer of thanks for the food, for good friends, and for his continued health, he answered. “I was telling R.C. about my plans for the property.”

Christie set her fork back down. She hoped he would not say he had decided to sell. “Yes?”

“You know that Cole brought out a new man to see me?” He scooped up a piece of beef and pie crust, chewing it before continuing. “Ooh we, Christie, this here is some right good eating. Yes, sirree bob.”

She leaned forward. “Yes, Kurt Matthews. I met him, too. He seems to be a nice guy, compared to the others, but looks can be deceiving.”

Pop patted her hand. “But we’ll be on the lookout, won’t we?”

“Yes. So, what did you think of him?”

Curtis finished chewing, then wiped his mouth before answering. “It was the funniest thing. He sat in the truck with his sunglasses on the entire time I spoke with Cole.” He shook his head and his mouth pushed over to the side as he thought. “I swear, he looks awfully familiar. Just can’t put my finger on it.”

“I thought the same thing.” She shrugged and

forked a piece of flaky potato before dipping it into the gravy.

Pop speared a tomato on his fork. "So, are ya selling, Curtis?"

"I already done told you, I'm not. So why are you asking—"

"That's what we thought, right Pop?" She didn't want them to start bickering.

Pop glanced at her before replying. "Um, yep. We thought so."

"Any more problems with Erik or Nick?" Christie wiped her mouth with a napkin.

Curtis sighed. "Those two are like a bad itch that won't go away. I don't know what to do, but I think I've figured it out—this way I'll respect my promise to their mother and not give them a thing."

"What do you have in mind?"

"I'm giving them each an acre."

"An acre? That's nothing, but they could still cause problems for you. Where is it?"

"Up next to your property on the back section."

"But unless they have permission for an egress,

they won't be able to get to it."

"I know." He grinned.

Pop guffawed. "You old coot, you outsmarted them good. They only have two ways in. Your property or ours and neither of us will give egress to it. They'll never be able to access it."

Christie waited. "You know they won't stand for that. I'm worried for you. They've already said they will take you to court to see about competency and giving them guardianship. This could help their case. Don't tell them about it. Let's think of something."

"Too late. I already told them. They were on their way to talk with Cole and that new guy, Kurt, about it."

Christie shook her head. "I don't like you being out here all alone. And now this. You've just been released from the hospital, and this will only add stress."

"Don't you worry none, hon. I have you two close by, if I need you." He wiped his mouth. "Now how about some of that caramel apple pie?"

After the dinner had ended, Christie and Pop rode back in the truck. "Pop, I don't think Curtis realizes how far people will go to get something they want. Cole as much as told me that Curtis wanted to know how much the property was worth, yet Curtis never said a word about it. So that makes me think maybe the boys had them go out there to try to get Curtis to sell."

Pop sucked on a toothpick. "Could be."

"That's it? Could be. Curtis almost died. I still have my doubts about it being an accident. His barn was on fire. Too many things trying to make him look like he's losing his mind. What's it going to take for you to realize how serious this is?"

He held up the toothpick. "Now, girly, I been around a while. I ain't stupid."

"I'm sorry, Pop. I didn't mean it that way." She gripped the steering wheel as they went around a large pothole.

"Let me finish. I ain't stupid, but I do see your point. I don't like what happened, and it worries me about them taking Curtis to court. I'm gonna have a heart-to-heart with him on our trip to the coast. Okay?"

"Yes, Pop. Thanks. I think it will make me feel better knowing no one can take that property away from Curtis."

The next morning Christie found a bunch of clothes and headed over to help Curtis with the scarecrow. After returning home, she headed over to Orchid's for tea and conversation. She stepped out of her truck just as a familiar white truck pulled up across the street. It was Kurt Matthews. She steeled herself for any confrontation and exited the truck.

Kurt spotted her, and after waving, he looked both ways before crossing the street. "Hello again. You're Miss Taylor, right?"

"Yes. I'm visiting Orchid."

He nodded. "Great. How are you and your father doing?"

"Fine."

"Cole told me about your dad and the truck hitting him."

It reminded Christie of the day that her father had been hit and how his shoulder and arm had broken from his fall. Even after all this time, it still caused him some issues with movement and ached when the weather changed.

Kurt continued. "He's lucky. That could have been serious."

"It was serious, but you're right, it could have been a lot worse. Thanks for asking."

"Well, it's important to know that, no matter what occurs in life, you have your faith to cling to when rough times happen."

Christie looked at the man intently. He looked to be sincere. Could the Websters have someone on staff that wasn't either a crook or a jerk? Truth be told, she'd let her faith slide after her mother's cancer. "Kurt, I recall you saying your daughter is living with you?"

He bowed his head. "Yes, sadly her husband was killed in Afghanistan. It was right about the time we moved back here—"

"Moved back here? I thought you hadn't lived here before."

"Oh, I've never lived here. My mother lived here many, many years ago. She lived with her folks in Waring." He frowned. "She was a great lady."

"Oh, sorry to hear—"

"Yes, it was everything at once. My son-in-law

getting killed, my mother passing, and this job offer." Something passed behind his eyes. "Strange timing, but mysterious ways and all that. Now I think I've seen why we're supposed to be here."

Christie wanted to ask more when the front door opened, and two little kids came running out the door yelling, "Grampa!" He quickly strode across to the yard and gathered the two children up into his arms. They hugged his neck, and he gave them big kisses on the cheeks.

"Well, as you can see, I have my hands full, so we'll have to cut our conversation short. Enjoy your time with Miss Merryweather. Tell her I said 'hi.'" He walked to the door where his daughter stood, watching them. She waved, and Christie waved back.

As Kurt set the children down, he turned back to Christie. "It'll all work out. Everything works to the good. Remember that." He went inside.

What is it about this guy? He reminds me so much of someone. But who?

Christie spent a wonderful afternoon with Orchid learning about weaving. Orchid said she'd even teach her if she wanted to learn. After setting up a time to meet again, Christie headed home, looking forward to a nice hot shower and a good movie. She knew Pop would be gone with Curtis fishing down at the coast. It would just be her at home for the next few days, and the realization of it was something she had been looking forward to for a while. Living by herself for a long time made that alone time more necessary. Pop was probably feeling it, too, after so many years on his own.

She was drifting off to sleep after binge-watching a show.

BANG!

Ugh, hunters. Can't they even wait until morning? This is unacceptable. I'm going to talk to Curtis about it when he gets back.

The following day, the guys arrived home, and after cleaning all the fish and shrimp, they held a fish fry and shrimp boil. The other guys who had been on the trip and their families had all come out to the house as they had a big outdoor kitchen in the back that made the cleaning and cooking much easier. Later after everyone had had their fill of fried fish and shrimp, they sat around talking and laughing until late in the evening. As everyone left that night, Christie thought about how precious the simple things in life were. Family, friends, and, yes, faith would get you through the toughest times. She went to bed contented.

It felt like she'd just closed her eyes when her phone rang. She snuck a look at the bedside clock. Nine in the morning. She must have been exhausted after last night's party. She answered the phone. "Hello?"

"Christie. Where are you?" Pop asked.

"What do you mean? I'm at home. In bed."

"I'll be home in five. Get ready. We have to go to Curtis's house. Now."

"Pop, what's happened?" She bolted upright at the tone of his voice.

"It's Curtis. He says he's killed someone."

Chapter Four

Christie grabbed her keys from the hook. Pop was already fidgeting next to her truck. "Hurry up!" He complained. "Why don't you just leave your keys in the truck?"

"Pop, I don't leave my keys in my vehicle. Now, let's focus on Curtis. What did he say?"

"Come now. I killed him."

Christie sighed. "That's it? Who did he kill?" She pushed down on the gas and made quick time over to the Altgelt ranch.

They pulled up to the old homestead and saw Curtis sitting on the porch steps, his head in his hands. Jumping quickly from the truck, Christie sprinted over to him. "Curtis, are you okay? What happened?"

The old man looked up; his tear-stained face had drained of any color. "I think I killed him. I must have done." He shook his head and cupped his face in his hands.

"Who? What do you mean you think you killed him?" She looked all around but saw no vehicle and no people. "Where is he?"

"It was the Grackles. They were sitting on the scarecrow. Taunting me. I was shooting at the birds." He looked past Christie; his gaze haunted with a picture she couldn't see. "I killed him. I killed him."

She stooped down in front of Curtis, hoping he hadn't had a mental breakdown. "Curtis, it's okay. You're okay. Let Pop take you inside, and I'll go check." She motioned for Pop to help, and together, they managed to steer Curtis up the steps and into the house.

"Pop," she grabbed his arm and whispered. "Please stay with him. He may have had an emotional break, don't leave him. I'll see what he thinks he did and come back."

Pop nodded and went over to where Curtis sat in his recliner, staring into space.

Christie walked around the house to the back where Curtis had said he'd shot someone. The day was still, and the only sound was the crunching underfoot of dry grass. She stepped on something and heard a crack. Bending down, she spied a broken pen, but the name was clear in its white lettering. Webster Realty. She reached for it but stepped back. Why would a pen from the real estate company be back here? As far as she knew, Curtis had never let Tyler or Emma come around the back of the house. Anyone could have one of those pens. As much as Erik and Nick worked with them, they probably had at least one of the pens. But that still didn't account for what it was doing here. Christie raised her hand to shield her eyes. She scanned the field and spied the scarecrow halfway down the rows of corn.

She steeled herself as she made her way to the scarecrow now on the ground. Straw lay strewn on the field from when they'd put it in the clothes to make the scarecrow. Bile rose in her throat, but she pushed past it to where Curtis had removed the headcloth with the painted smile on the front. A jolt shot through her body.

It was Kurt Matthews.

After the sheriff arrived, and EMT's had cared for

Curtis, Pop and Christie were allowed to return home. Neither spoke. The shock of it all still too new, too fresh on their minds. At home, Christie put on the coffeepot. Pop came in and sat at the dining table.

"Pop, I—"

"Christie, I love ya darling, but I just need some time to think."

She nodded, left the kitchen, and walked outside. As she thought of the Matthews family, she realized that, yet another tragedy had struck their loved ones. How would they cope with yet one more loss? She needed to speak to someone. Instinctively, she pushed in the number as her phone rang at the same moment.

Orchid calming voice came through the phone, "The police are across the street. What do you need, child?"

Christie stifled a sob. She'd always heard about people who were empaths. "I don't know. How did you know to call me?"

"I always listen to my gut. When I feel I should do something, I do it. It said to call you. I gather this has something to do with all the mess you've told me about. Now you don't need to be driving right now. You stay home and visit me tomorrow morning. I only met Mr. Matthews a few times, but he was a good man. My heart is breaking for his sweet family."

After they'd said goodbye, Christie went inside and poured coffee into a mug. Her father was no longer in the kitchen. Instead, he sat outside on the front porch, rocking. Mutt and Jeffrey stared at him intently, as if the dogs could read the emotion in their master. Finally, Jeffrey picked himself up and laid his chocolate-colored head on Pop's arm. Pop stopped rocking and absently stroked the animal's head.

"This will kill Curtis." He stared ahead as he spoke.

"Pop, it's not his fault. He didn't put Kurt there and then shoot him."

"I know that. You know that. But who else knows that?"

"What do you mean?" She took a sip of the hot coffee.

"I mean someone had to know that Curtis would shoot his rifle at the birds. They don't care about scarecrows. They'll sit on your head if they want to."

He sighed. "I mean someone wanted to cause problems for Curtis."

"Well, we know his sons do, but what about Kurt? Why him? What was he doing out at Curtis's place?"

"That's a good question and one we'll never know the answer to now." He shook his head. "I'm real tired, hon. I'm going to go watch some television."

Christie waited until she could hear the soft snores coming from Pop's chair. She needed to clear her head, and what better way than to go for a ride? Changing into jeans and boots, Christie pulled a hat on before walking to the barn. As she approached, Champ walked toward her.

"Hey fella." He nuzzled her. "How about a ride?" She opened the gate, and he followed her to where the tack sat ready for use. Christie picked up the currycomb and stroked the horse with it, then followed it with the hard brush and finally the soft brush. She also combed his mane and tail.

Confident that Champ was ready to be saddled, Christie first checked his feet with a hoof pick, then placed the saddle on his back. Finally, she put the bridle on him. She led him into the yard, Mutt and Jeffrey following close by with tails wagging. They wanted to come along, too.

Christie reached down and patted the labs on the head. “Okay, you can come, but try to keep up.”

She mounted Champ, and they set off at a slow pace until they had cleared the rocky bluff area. Christie then squeezed her legs telling Champ to canter. The ride was good for her, and she thought of nothing but the connection between horse and rider. After a while, she slowed Champ back down, and the foursome made it home as dusk descended.

“I figured you were out riding. Nothing better to clear your head than to get out by yourself.” Pop leaned against a barn post. Mutt and Jeffrey shot up to the water bowls and lapped hungrily at the water.

Christie dismounted and walked Champ over to the trough to drink. “What are you thinking about for dinner?”

“Not sure. We can talk about it when you’re done.”

“Sounds good.”

She walked Champ for a bit more before hitching

him to a post. She removed the bridle and saddle and used a wet brush. After she'd completed brushing him, she picked up the sweat scraper and worked her way down his body. After checking his hooves again, she led him to a stall and made sure he had fresh hay, oats, and water. Once he entered the stall, she produced an apple for him. Christie had cut it in half, and as he chewed one piece of it, she stroked his muzzle. Then she fed him the other half before going to her saddle and wiping it down.

Back in the house, she took a shower and put on fresh clothing. "Pop, do you want to go out and eat somewhere, or should we do something simple, like sandwiches?"

He was watching Chuck Norris on the television.

She continued, "Or I could go get us something and bring it back?"

"I'm not hungry. You can get something if you want." He went back to watching the martial arts cowboy combination.

Christie had an idea. She punched in the number. "Orchid, how would you like to go out to dinner? My treat." After getting a confirmation on the other end, she leaned down and kissed Pop. "Do you want me to bring you anything?"

"Nah, I'm good. You kids have a good time." He waved goodbye.

Christie chuckled. Neither she nor Orchid were kids by any means. But before that, she stopped by HEB and picked up flowers and a condolence card for the Matthews. Even though she'd only just met Kurt, she felt it was the neighborly thing to do.

Arriving at Orchid's, she saw cars parked up and down the block. Christie didn't want to intrude, so she left the items in the truck. Mrs. Matthews was hugging someone at the door at the same time she spied Christie.

"Hello!" The woman called out to her.

Christie stopped and waited as the woman approached. "Hi, I'm Carole. Kurt's wife. I heard that you..."she caught her breath "you're the one who found him."

She nodded. "Yes. I'm so sorry, Mrs. Matthews. I had only spoken with him a few times but—"

Carole pulled a tissue from her pocket and wiped her nose, already raw and red from crying. "Thank you. It's such a shock." She turned back to the house. "As you can see, we have a full house, but could you come by tomorrow and talk to me?"

"I'm not sure I have—"

"Please." The woman clung to Christie's arm.

"Sure. Of course."

The woman wiped her eyes. "Thank you." She walked toward the house, then turned back. "I think when I show you what I found, you may have a different opinion about Mr. Altgelt's guilt."

Christie watched as the woman made her way back into the house. What was it that she could say that would change her opinion? There was no way that Curtis had meant to kill Kurt. There was nothing Christie could envision that would cause Curtis to have done anything to a man he didn't know—or even one he knew. Her thoughts wandered to the scene. Someone had put Kurt into the scarecrow's clothes and covered his face. Also, there'd been no blood at the scene, so it meant Kurt had been dead before Curtis had shot at the "scarecrow," knocking it to the ground. Someone wanted to make it look like Curtis had killed Kurt, but the question of why kept repeating in her mind. What would someone have to gain by Kurt's death?

The reason was clear. With Curtis out of the way and on trial for murder, that would easily clear the path for his stepsons to move ahead with their plans to take over the property. At least, she was thankful Curtis had an airtight alibi since he'd been fishing at the coast with Pop and other guys from their men's group.

First thing's first, she needed to convince Curtis to get a gate put up on his property. She feared for his safety more than ever. Christie determined she'd get Pop to speak to Curtis about the gate.

Chapter Five

After calling Pop, she added two barbecue orders to go. Pop had returned to be with Curtis now that the crime scene techs had left. Christie wanted to have a better look around the place and see if there was anything she'd missed before.

Arriving at the house, Christie left the barbecue with the men and strode out to the back. What had once been Curtis's cornfield was now a destroyed and trampled mess of bent and broken stalks. A section of it was cordoned off with yellow caution tape and the boards that had held the scarecrow up had been removed. The only sign of where it had been was the hole where the post had stood.

Someone must have killed Kurt, then brought his body here. They probably hadn't expected Curtis to shoot at the Grackles. But Kurt had just moved here. Was he an innocent person who had been in the wrong place at the wrong time? Yet, his wife had alluded to some information that could show Curtis had intentionally killed Kurt. That made no sense. She needed to get back over to the Matthews house and find out what Kurt's wife meant by her statement.

For now, that would have to wait. She returned to the house where the men sat eating brisket sandwiches. Christie noticed how pale and even more frail Curtis had become. She finally broached the subject.

"Curtis, I think it might be a good idea for you to get a gate like Pop and I have. The developers have stopped showing up unexpectedly, and it's made it much nicer knowing who is able to come and go on the property."

Curtis shook his head. "Never thought I'd see the day when I couldn't simply live on my own property without living in a prison."

"It's not—"

"It is," he chided. "I've lived here pretty much my entire life. Why should I have to change the way I come and go now? Who knows how much longer I'll be here?"

Christie sighed. "I'm not trying to make things hard on you. I just want to make sure you're safe. The accident you had is too much of a coincidence for my liking. You could have easily died out there without us finding you when we did. Now this. It's obvious someone is trying to frame you for Kurt's murder. I know you and Pop are tough old birds, but please, at least consider adding a gate to keep people who mean you harm off the property."

He sighed and rubbed his weather-beaten, rough, and bruised hands over a torn paper napkin. "How about this? I promise to give it some thought."

"That works." Christie turned to Pop. "See you later at the house?"

He nodded. "Me and Curtis are gonna go talk to Hug."

Christie smiled at the nickname given to Hugh, now Sheriff Clauson, when he was younger. "You know he can't tell you anything."

"I've known him since he was knee high to a grasshopper. We need some answers."

Poor Hug. He wouldn't know what hit him when

these two got together. "Okay, well, I'll leave you to it. Just be nice. I don't want to have to come bail you all out of jail." She kissed Pop on his cheek. For now, she needed to see if she could speak to Mrs. Matthews.

The next day, Christie drove over to the Matthews house. Lana, Kurt's daughter answered the door. Christie expressed her sympathies and asked if Mrs. Matthews was able to speak with her.

"Let me see if my mom's available. Please, come in." The young woman motioned to Christie with a half-hearted smile. Christie noted her puffy eyes and dark bags, contrary to that the brave face she was trying to portray. Inside the house, a small living area was tidy and held only a large brown sectional, a television mounted to the wall, and a box overflowing with toys.

Mrs. Matthews entered from the hall, placing a finger to her lips. "The children are down for their nap. We can go in the kitchen." She led the way into the small kitchen Christie recalled from when Hector had lived there. Christie noted that they had removed a bank of cabinets that had stood as a pantry so that there was more space for the table. However, the room remained tiny and cramped.

"Please, sit down." The woman gestured to a chair which Christie took. "Iced tea?"

"Yes, thank you."

Lana said, "Mom, sit down, and I'll take care of it."

Mrs. Matthews sat and took a deep breath, pursing her lips together in a tight smile that didn't reach her eyes. "Thank you for coming. I really didn't know who to go to with this, but Miss Merryweather said I should speak with you." She wrung her hands and fought for composure as tears welled in her eyes. "Sorry, it just comes on whenever it wants to."

"Please, Mrs. Matthews, don't apologize. I worked as a hospice nurse, so I'm very familiar with grief." She nodded her thanks as the young woman sat a glass of iced tea in front of Christie and her mother.

The woman ran her finger up and down the glass wiping away the condensation that had already formed. "Call me Carole."

"Sorry, old habits." Christie took a sip of the sweet brew, waiting for the woman to compose herself.

Finally, Carole took a deep breath before speaking. "We moved here because of a job opportunity for Kurt. At least, that's what I thought. He told me this was a great position and that it would help all of us. This house was to be temporary as we searched for our own place with a bit of land and a place for my daughter, Lana, and the children to be nearby." She grabbed at a tissue from a box on the table and wiped her eyes. "That's what he had led me to believe. But Kurt had a different reason for coming here." She wrung her hands together.

Carole nodded at Lana, who retrieved a shoebox from on top of the refrigerator. After looking at her mother, who assented with a quick nod, Lana set the box down in front of Christie.

"Open it." Mrs. Matthews cupped her hands over her mouth.

Christie's mind went to Pandora, and she steadied herself as she lifted the lid off the box. Inside, a ribbon held a bunch of yellowed envelopes together. She set those to the side as Carole led her to one particular document. It was a birth certificate. On it, Kurt's name was written, as well as his mother's name, and in the box for father, they had left it blank. Her brow furrowed, and she looked up at the woman. "Turn the letters over and remove the ribbon." Carole pointed to them.

Christie did as instructed and noted that the letters had been written on the front. The sender's name was either absent, scratched out, or cut off. Each letter had been written on with a date on the right side, and she saw that someone had placed the letters in order. "I'm not sure I understand." She looked up at the woman staring intently at her over the table.

"We didn't, either, at first. But look at the diary. There's a page that's marked. Christie took the diary and opened it to the bookmarked page.

Cursive writing was hard to read in some parts as it was plain from the pages that the person had been crying as they wrote.

Should I have told him? It's too late. I've lived with it this long. It would just cause more harm than good now. But I know my time is short. —no easy answers. -urt, I'll always love you.

Christie looked up. “Told who? And told him what? She says she loved Kurt.”

“That’s what we thought at first, too. But the first letter is smeared. We thought the letter was a K but it’s probably C. Here, look back at his birth certificate. His given name was Kurt Alton.”

“Okay,” Christie said, then stopped. She started.

“I see that you understand now. Kurt Alton. Curtis Altgelt.”

Christie shook her head. “So that’s why Kurt looked so familiar to me. He was Curtis’s son. But if Kurt knew—”

“That’s what we wondered. Why didn’t he confront his father? We think he wanted to make sure before he said anything to him. That’s why he jumped at the chance to go with Cole out to the property.”

“But he never got out of the truck.” Christie continued, “He knew Curtis would be able to see his own likeness staring back at him.”

“What was he planning on doing?” She took another sip of tea.

“I know he would speak with Tyler about it. He

went there, but when he arrived, the two stepsons were at the office. He didn't want them to know about his possible connection to Curtis. At least at that point."

"Do you know if they found out he was Curtis's son? That would technically make him the rightful heir to the property and at least cut Erik and Nick's portion to a third. Plus, if Kurt didn't like the idea of selling to the Websters, that could have caused more problems."

"I'd never thought of that. The Websters would wonder if Kurt would support them or Curtis." She shook her head, and tears spilled down her cheeks. "All I know is someone killed my husband, and I'm not letting them get away with it. Even if it was his father."

Christie sat back in her chair. "Curtis would never do something like that. What would he stand to gain from it?"

Anger born from grief filled Carole's voice. "All I know is this. They found Kurt dead on his property. The bullets they found match Curtis's gun. The wounds match Curtis's gun. He even said he shot at the scarecrow. That's a confession right there! Kurt worked for the people who we now know are trying to pressure Curtis to sell his property. Someone had to drive him there. They found his vehicle parked on the side of the road where no one would see who he left with. It must have been someone he knew or wanted to talk with for him to get in the other vehicle. His last call to me was when he saw a vehicle approaching." She leaned forward on the table. "He said it was Curtis."

"That's impossible. Curtis was with my Pop and other men down at the coast fishing."

Carole sat back in her chair and crossed her arms. "Are you sure?"

A sudden thought crossed Christie's mind. The sound of a gun blast the other night. No. That timeframe didn't work. Curtis wasn't home then. "When was the call from Kurt?"

"It was—wait, let me look." Carole left the room, then returned with her phone. Christie waited as she scrolled back through the calls. "Here it is. Nine-forty-five." She sat the phone on the table and clasped her hands together. "He'd been acting strange for a few days, and after I confronted him about it, he told me he thought Curtis Altgelt was his father. Curtis had said he'd meet him that evening." She stifled a sob. "That's the last time I spoke with him."

"Mom." The young woman sprang from her chair and cradled her mother as she wept softly.

Christie rose. "I'm so sorry for your loss. Truly. But Curtis was with my father and some other men fishing down at Padre. There's no way he met Kurt that night."

The woman sniffed and wiped at her reddened face. "I know what Kurt told me. As he signed off, he said 'here he comes.' Are you willing to stand behind your statement? I know he told me the truth."

At a loss for words, Christie bid the pair goodbye. She knew one thing for certain. She had to speak to Pop and to Curtis. Someone was lying.

Chapter Six

Christie arrived home to an excited pair of dogs. Mutt and Jeffrey sprung from their spots on the front porch, running down to meet her, their tails wagging so hard, that their entire back-ends danced with delight. She bent down and rubbed each of their heads. "Yes, I've missed you guys too. What's it been—a few hours? Lifetime, am I right?" She laughed, and they continued with their show of happiness toward her. A whistle snapped the pair to attention.

"You boys leave that girl alone. Let her at least get away from the truck," Pop yelled toward them.

The dogs backed up, and Christie made her way to the porch, her adoring entourage following close at her heels.

"Hey, Pop." She brushed his cheek with her lips. "Listen, I need to talk to you about the trip to Padre with Curtis and the guys."

"Ask away, girlie. Just know I can't share

everything." He winked.

"I'm sure it was tons of wine, women, and—"

Pop laughed. "Okay, you got me there. Those days are long gone for our group, though we do have some younger guys who tagged along. Even Mike came for a bit."

She knew that, by younger guys, Pop was referring to men in their fifties. Mike was father to Jess, a teenager who would come to live with her and Pop the following year once Mike went back to work in the oil fields.

"He is still thanking me—us—for taking Jess in so he can finish his senior year here." He smiled.

"Pop, I really need to ask you more about Curtis than about the actual trip, so your guy secrets are safe."

"You don't have a good look on your face, and that tone sounds ominous. Let's get us a drink, and you can tell me what's troubling ya, darling."

After they each had a large sweet tea in hand, they strolled out to the porch and took seats in the rockers. "So, what's on your mind?" Pop took a sip of the cold brew.

"Pop, when you guys were fishing, um, was there any time that Curtis wasn't with you?"

"Wasn't with us? What do you mean by that?" His brow furrowed as his gaze narrowed.

"Okay. Look, here's the thing. I visited Kurt's wife, and she says that Curtis met Kurt the night he was killed. She suspects Curtis of killing him."

"Whoa. That's some story there, missy. Why in the world would she ever suspect Curtis of something horrible like that? Plus, Curtis didn't even know Kurt. So, Curtis just killed a man he doesn't know? For what reason?"

"How about because Kurt was his son." Christie waited for Pop's response.

"His son?" Pop spoke aloud to himself. "He does bear a resemblance to Curtis, now that I think of it." He shook his head. "It would thrill Curtis to have a son. Nope, makes no sense."

"What if that son worked for a developer who wanted to buy his land? From what Curtis has said in the past, he doesn't want that land built on, even after he's gone. He would know the only thing standing in the way of that was his rightful heir, who could do with the land as he pleased."

Pop swiveled in his chair, anger punctuated his voice. "You mean to tell me that you think Curtis is capable of murder because he wants to protect land that's been in his family for generations?"

"I'm not saying that. I'm just thinking aloud here. His alibi is being with you all down in Padre. I want to be able to tell her there's no way it was Curtis who Kurt met that evening."

Pop took a sip and sat silent for a moment. He stared off across the land, and Christie noted his expression was one of deep thought.

"What is it Pop? I know you're thinking of something and you're not telling me."

"I don't like telling tales out of school." He sighed. "But truth be told, I can't say for certain that Curtis was there all the time."

"What do you mean?" She shifted in her chair and waited for his answer.

"We had an early dinner as some of the guys were going out for overnight fishing. Others were going out to the docks, and some were heading off to watch sports. Curtis said he was tired, so we dropped him off back at the house."

"When's the next time you saw him?"

"Early the next morning. I got up, and he was in the kitchen making coffee. When I told him he looked plum-worn-out, he said he'd been up all night fishing. Since everyone had their favorite spots, he could have been anywhere." Pop shook his head. "I do recall asking what he'd caught, and it took him a minute before he said he'd fallen asleep, so he'd caught nothing."

"Did he have his truck down there?"

"No. We rode in mine."

Christie smiled. "Good, then he couldn't have come back."

Pop stroked his scratchy beard. "Well, actually, he could have done. I left my keys on the chest in our bedroom and went off with the other guys."

"Did you get any gas on the way?"

"Nope. Filled up and did not need to get more."

Christie got up from her chair and went to the

truck. She yelled back, "How many miles to Padre?"

Pop stood and set the glass of tea on the railing. "Let's see. I think two hundred, maybe two-thirty. Why?"

"If you didn't get gas after you filled up here, then it should show around four hundred miles on your truck." She opened the door and got in. The trip odometer read over eight hundred miles. Christie gripped the wheel and rested her head on her hands. It was only a few hours back to Comfort, and Curtis could have easily taken the truck with no one noticing it was gone during that timeframe. He had probably refilled the gas but hadn't thought of the trip odometer. Then, he just slept in the truck or went out and acted like he'd fished all night along with the others.

Pop watched as Christie came back to the porch. "He wouldn't, Christie. I know him."

"Well, it looks like you don't know him well enough. We need to talk with him right away."

After they'd called Curtis, Pop and Christie drove over to the Altgelt ranch. When they pulled up, a frail-looking man greeted them with a simple nod. Christie saw that he hadn't shaved in a while, his hair was disheveled, and it looked like he'd slept in his clothes.

"Come in." He motioned.

All three went into the kitchen and sat at the table. The silence and emotion filled the air, with no one wanting to speak first.

"Look, Curtis. We—"

Curtis stopped Pop from speaking. "I have to get this off my chest. I figure you two are here because you want to know about what I'm going to say. Am I right?"

"Possibly."

"I got a call from Kurt. He told me he thought I was his father. I thought he was crazy. But then, he told me who his mother was." He stopped speaking, fighting back emotion. "I'm not proud of it, but we met—and, well, things happened." He stood and paced the floor. "But she never told me. I would have married her. We'd been writing, and I told her that I'd received a scholarship to A&M. I'd be the first one in my family to graduate high school, much less attend college. My parents were over the moon." He waved his hand.

"Hold on." He left the room.

While he was gone, Christie ran hot water in the sink and added soap. She gathered the dirty dishes and scraped them into the wastebasket before adding them to the sink. She'd cleaned off the table and put on coffee by the time Curtis reappeared. In his hands, he held a stack of lavender envelopes. They reminded Christie of the pile Carole had shown her.

"As I said, we wrote all the time. She had gone to visit relatives over the summer after we graduated. After I told her about the scholarship, this was the last letter I received." He handed Christie a letter. She looked at the date stamp. It must have been shortly after she'd found out she was pregnant.

Dear Curtis,

So happy to hear about your scholarship. I know your parents are proud, and so am I. Enjoy your time at school.

I hate to tell you this way, but I've met someone. He's a great guy, and I'm not sure it would be proper to continue our correspondence. Please know that your love and friendship has meant everything to me.

Love Always, L

"Now I know. You see. She knew if she'd told me about being pregnant that I wouldn't have gone to college. I wouldn't have met Marilyn, rest her soul. I loved Marilyn and still do, but I never got over Lorinda. I truly believe we were soulmates." He struggled to keep his composure. "She never told me. All these years, I had a son. A son." Curtis took in a deep breath. I need to go outside for a minute. "R.C., join me."

Christie watched from the window as the two elderly men, who had been friends since their youth, walked out toward the field. Pop reached over and squeezed Curtis on the shoulder. Christie's eyes welled up with tears as she could see the struggle Curtis was having to hold it together emotionally. She set to work on the dishes and waited for the men to return. Once they came inside, Curtis was more composed. The time spent with Pop must have helped to steady him. She poured out coffee for them and sat. When everyone was settled, she spoke.

"According to Carole, Kurt called her around nine

thirty the evening he went missing. Can you fill us in on that?"

Curtis nodded. "He'd called me that day. Wanted to meet and see if I'd consent to a DNA test. I told him I'd be glad to meet with him. Kurt wanted to meet that day. Said he had something important to tell me that he'd found out."

"What was it?"

"He wouldn't tell me. He said it was something he found while doing some research on properties and such. He wanted to talk with me about it, but now—"

"So, you took Pop's truck and drove it back to meet him?"

"Yep. We'd had dinner, and I knew everyone would be so busy, they wouldn't notice me gone. Three hours up and back would be easy." He looked at the pair. "What gave me away? I refilled the truck to the amount of gas in the tank."

"Pop always resets the trip odometer when he fills gas. Life-long habit," Christie replied.

Curtis nodded. "Yep, I was so busy worrying about the gas and getting back in time, I didn't think about the trip odometer. Guess I'll never make it in a life of crime."

"So, you drove back up here and met Kurt that night?"

"Yes. He was waiting down the road. I pulled up, and he followed me out to the house. He showed me his birth certificate and his mom's letters. I could see by looking at him that he had Altgelt blood in him. I didn't know if he was telling me because he wanted to get his hands on the property."

"Did you feel that was his intention?"

"No. In fact, he said he thought the property should stay wild, as there was no need for it to be built up. He said Cole had brought him out, and he'd seen how beautiful and peaceful the place was."

Pop spoke up. "I bet that didn't sit well with them Websters."

"You'd think. But he had said nothing to them about being kin."

"Hmmm, could they have overheard anything?" Christie grabbed the coffeepot for refills, but both Curtis and Pop declined.

"I guess they could have, but I'm not sure how." He sipped the final dregs from his cup.

Christie asked, "What about Erik and Nick? That could really ruin their plans."

He nodded. "That's what concerns me. What if Kurt told Erik and Nick that they could be half-brothers? They were already thinking they were the only two who would inherit."

"It also gives them significant motive to see him gone." Christie took the cups and placed them in the cooling dishwater. "I wouldn't put anything past those two."

Curtis replied, "Yep. As much as I hate to say it, I have to agree with you."

Pop sat back in the chair and crossed his arms. "You met Kurt out here, then what happened?"

"Let's see. Um, oh. A raccoon was trying to get into the chicken coop. I grabbed my gun and took a shot at it. It was dark, so didn't hit it, but I scared it off."

"What time was that?"

"I dunno. Elevenish?"

"Okay. I heard a shot, but I think it was closer to

morning. I remember because it irritated me that hunters were starting so early. But I don't know what time it was, since I didn't look at the clock."

"Back to your story. Then what happened?" Pop gestured for Curtis to continue.

"We just talked a bit about his family, and we made plans to meet again when I came back from the trip. He agreed, and that's when he told me he had some important information, but it could wait for a few days. I walked him to his truck, and I got in your truck and headed back to Padre."

Christie interjected. "Where did you leave your gun?"

"Like I always do. On the rack. Inside."

"And the house was locked?"

"I don't lock the house."

Christie had known Curtis would say that, but she wanted to confirm it. "So, basically, anyone could have entered your house and used your home phone to lure Kurt back out here. Then, it was easy to use your gun." She shivered. "It also means someone knew Kurt was meeting you that night. They planned it out. Get rid of

Kurt. Frame you. We know of at least two people who want you out of the picture. We just have to decide if they're willing to kill for it."

Chapter Seven

When Curtis refused to come back to the house with them, they ensured that he would be extra-vigilant. Anything at all suspicious, he was to contact Pop or Christie immediately.

As they drove home, Christie expressed her concern. “Pop, this is serious. First, I believe they tried to kill Curtis by digging that hole and setting up that rock cairn. Anyone who would have tripped would have landed on the rock and could have been killed outright. Now this. I don’t like Nick or Erik, but I can’t see them do something like this. We need to find out where they were on the night Kurt was murdered.”

“Agree. How do you propose to do that?”

“Well, as much as I hate to, I could go down to the Websters and listen to what they have to say about selling our property. That would give me an excuse to ask questions about Erik and Nick and thoughts about his place.”

"I dunno. I'm not crazy on you getting mixed up with those folk if they had something to do with it. Maybe I should come along with you."

"No. They know you're set against it. I can make out more that I've been considering it and how I might convince you."

Pop rubbed his scraggly beard, the scratching sound loud in the quiet. "Okay, but only to help Curtis. I don't want to have to come up there and—"

"I'll be careful. Do you know if Erik and Nick are still here? Last I heard, I thought they were headed back to Dallas."

"No, they're still here. I've seen Nick's Mercedes when I've gone into town for supplies." He wiped down his mustache. "Also, Curtis has to get the other horses back. They're bringing them to our place." He gazed at Christie and held up his hands. "I know. I know. It's a lot of work. But if we need to, we can hire some kids from 4H to help."

"I certainly understand wanting to help Curtis, but I still can't believe he didn't have insurance."

"I guess he didn't think about it. He just has

insurance on the house."

Christie turned off the truck ignition and sat back. "What? Pop, I thought you said he didn't have any insurance."

"Turns out, he does. It's an older policy that just comes out of his bank account automatically. His house is paid off, so I guess he forgot about it. But it's just for the house."

"We need to check it out because it's usually outbuildings, too, which would mean enough money to rebuild his barn. Then his horses could be brought back there. Though, I don't know if Curtis can care for them either."

Pop patted her hand. "One thing at a time, girly." He swung out of the truck, then turned around. "Now, let's think of something better like when we can start cutting wood for your house. Looking forward to getting my girl her own place and setting down roots."

She climbed out of the cab and went around the truck. "You're just wanting me out of the house."

"That, too." He winked at her.

Christie thought through her plan for the evening

to visit the Webster offices in the morning. Then, she'd called Orchid and invited her to join her for lunch. Orchid had agreed, and they'd decided on a later lunch so they could go into San Antonio and stroll along the Riverwalk.

In the morning, Christie pulled her hair back into clips, the soft curls still damp from the shower. She'd given up trying to dry her hair since it would frizz, and even the supposed "curly girl" methods seemed to be more trouble than they were worth. She applied a moisturizer with sunscreen to her face. Even with a bit of tint in it, she knew it wouldn't hide the freckles that had become more prominent since moving back to Texas. She approached the mirror over the dresser and swiped on a coral lip stain. Sitting on the bed, Christie grabbed her nice pair of turquoise Lucchese boots. She'd treated herself to the pair upon returning to Texas, and she received compliments on them whenever she wore them. She wore a simple russet slip dress with a low-slung turquoise and dark chocolate belt. Adding a pair of feathered earrings, she felt confident and ready to do battle with the Websters.

Christie walked out to the back where Pop was letting the horses out into the paddock. "I'm leaving, Pop. Wish me luck."

"No luck needed with my girl. Spine of steel, just like your mama, God rest her soul." He opened another door, and Champ trotted out into the yard. He ambled over to her.

"Hey, there, good-looking. Maybe we can get in a ride tomorrow." The horse thrust its muzzle in the air as if it were nodding its head in agreement.

Christie leaned over and kissed Pop on the cheek. "I'm not sure when I'll be back, Pop. After I visit with them, Orchid is joining me for lunch in San Antonio. It's such a nice day, we're going to stroll around the Riverwalk and possibly stop by the McNay. They have a fiber exhibit Orchid's been wanting to see."

"Okay, sounds good. I'll probably head over to Curtis's and spend some time with him."

"Good idea. I don't like him being out there all alone. Plus, get him to look for that insurance. That could make a huge difference if it covered him for the barn fire."

Christie drove into town. She parked on Main Street and made her way to Webster Realty. Taking a deep breath and steeling herself for the meeting, she entered. Inside, a receptionist sat at a desk typing away on a computer. When Christie entered, the woman rose from her seat. "Hello!" she chirped. "Welcome to Webster Realty. I'm Lisa. How may I help you?"

Christie shook the woman's outstretched hand. "Hi, Lisa. I'm afraid I don't have an appointment, but I was wondering if I could speak to one of the Webster's about our property."

The woman came around the desk. "You're in luck. They've both arrived and are in the back. If you'll just have a seat, I can let them know you're here and see if they have time to meet you. If not, I'm sure Cole or Albert—"

"I'd prefer to meet with the Websters. If I need to make an appointment to come back, then I'm happy to do that." Christie knew she wouldn't have to worry about the Websters not seeing her but wanted to cover her bases just in case.

"Great. Coffee, water, soda?" The young woman

replied.

"I'm fine right now. Thank you." She stayed standing as the woman went down a long hall and knocked on a back door.

She hadn't waited long before the always effervescent Emma appeared from the back room. "Miss Taylor. How nice to see you." She held out her hand and shook Christie's. Since the last time Christie had seen her, she'd had her long, blonde hair cut into a slick bob.

"Cute haircut," Christie responded.

"Thank you." Emma ran her manicured red nails down the glossy blow-out. "I thought it was time for a change."

"Ms. Taylor." A man's deep voice stopped their exchange.

Christie watched as Tyler headed toward them, a cup with the Webster logo in his hand. "I didn't know if you had time to see me, or if I need to make an appointment."

"Of course not. We would love to speak with you," he responded.

Emma smiled. "How about we go into the conference room?" She waved toward a door with her hand before turning to Lisa. "No interruptions."

"Yes, Mrs. Webster." The woman went back to typing.

"Please." Tyler stood to the side to allow Christie to enter a room, tastefully decorated in blues, whites, and reds—Texan and American colors. The walls were covered in pictures of McMansions and blueprints with a bookcase along the back wall filled with awards from the Parade of Homes, real estate, and other entities. In the middle, a large carved wooden owl sat on a pedestal.

Christie chose a seat close to the door. She knew she would want a quick exit if they didn't provide any information.

Emma sat on one side and Tyler on her other side. Emma said, "Did Lisa offer you something to drink?"

"Yes, I'm fine. I don't want to take up too much of your time. It's only..." She steeled herself and hoped she could pull off the interview. This is for Curtis. She raised her head. "I feel a bit funny being here," she began. That part was true at least. “After seeing Curtis struggling and my Pop getting older, I’m just wondering about, well, maybe, selling a portion of the land so as to ensure my father’s care.” She hoped her hesitancy at telling something untrue came out as nervousness.

“Of course. You want to do what’s best for your father. It just makes sense. It would provide you with the means to take care of him and make sure that you are taken care of, too.” Tyler smiled, but Christie felt more unease than before.

“It’s just, I’m not sure what portions to even consider selling. I know Pop would want to keep a large amount of property around the homestead and not be able to see any development.”

Tyler pushed back his chair and excused himself. As they waited, Emma and Christie talked about the weather and other things people talk about with strangers. A knock on the door sounded. Albert, Emma’s brother, stuck his head in the door. “Oh, sorry. Didn’t mean to interrupt. I wanted to ask a question about a closing, but I can catch you later.”

"Albert, I think you've met Miss Taylor." Emma motioned to Christie.

He stepped into the room. "Yes. Nice to see you again." He tipped his felt hat and exited the room as Tyler returned with a rolled-up paper, which Christie knew would most likely show their property and the Altgelt ranch.

Tyler unrolled it and folded it backward, then held it down with his hand and a long piece of wood he retrieved from the bookcase.

"Here's your property." He pointed at the area.

Christie stood up, and Emma followed, so they were all now standing over the plans. "Is this the Altgelt ranch?" Christie knew it was, but she wanted to have them show her.

"Yes. Here's his house." Tyler pointed at an outline on the map.

"Just curious but how many miles is it from this spot on our property to this spot on the Altgelt ranch."

"Sure." Tyler pulled out a ruler and measured. "Looks like approximately seventy acres. I think it's about forty of the Altgelt land and about thirty on yours. That would be a good amount for you and your Pop's care."

Christie sat back down and acted like she was thinking about it. "Yes, but that would only be if Curtis sells off part of his property. That way, the outer edges would stay wild and create a barrier with any development in the middle."

Tyler joined her and sat facing her. "Not to worry about that. Can I share something with you? In confidence?"

Christie nodded, hoping he would give her the information she needed.

"We've been talking to his sons. They're worried about his mental capacity. He's been having lots of problems lately aside from his physical accidents. Now, with him having shot someone, the boys are in a better position to gain conservatorship of the property."

"Yes, I've been worried about Curtis." That much at least would be true. They always said to stick to the truth as much as possible. "He's told me about things happening he can't explain."

Tyler retorted, “That’s why it would help him, too. He’ll have plenty of money, and he can have a nice spot in a nursing home where he’s cared for twenty-four/seven.”

“So, you’re saying they are planning on selling the entire property?”

Emma spoke up. “No, we’re simply saying that options are on the table. I think if he knew y’all would sell a portion of your land, it might help him sell off a portion of his land. That way it would be a win-win for everyone!”

“I’m not sure. You know my father is dead set against selling off any of the property. He wouldn’t want any large development next to us.”

Emma started to speak, but with a quick shake of the head from Tyler, remained silent.

Tyler said, “We’re thinking five to ten acre plots for sale. We’ve left this large swatch of trees here, so you’d never even see the subdivision.”

“Subdivision?” Christie knew that meant a lot more homes.

“Just a figure of expression.” He smiled at her.

"Again, it's not in my name, and I doubt Pop will go for it." She exhaled and waited.

"Don't worry about that. Tyler is helping Nick and Erik, and he can probably help you, too." Emma beamed. "He's so good at getting things done."

"Really? How?" Christie turned to Tyler. This is what she needed to know. What were Nick and Erik doing behind Curtis's back?

"It's nothing, really. I simply gave them some advice. When you have an elderly person who is becoming senile, you can get a court to provide you with guardianship over their affairs. That way you can ensure that what is in the best interest of that person happens without having to go through them." He rolled up the plans. "I'm not telling you to do anything like that."

"Of course not," Christie replied to him. He was telling her that he could help remove her father from control of the property. She thought Erik and Nick were bad, but this guy was a snake in the grass. "If I decided it would be best to sell a portion of the property, there could be a way to skirt around my father's control over it. I'd just need to find a lawyer that could help with that."

"Is your father having any memory problems? Putting things in the wrong place? Forgetting things? Anything that could be harmful to himself or others?"

"Now that you mention it, on my last visit we had a fire in the kitchen. I think he left a pot on the stove, and if I hadn't come home when I did, who knows what would have happened?"

"Exactly. You only want what's best for your father, correct?"

Boy, this guy was playing her like a fiddle. He was good at saying everything without saying anything that might implicate himself in any fashion.

"Of course. He may need care, and I won't be able to do it all the time."

"Exactly. Listen, why don't you think about it and how we can work together to ensure your father has everything he needs for the rest of his life?" He pulled an embossed leather case from his pocket and held out his card. "Here's my business card. I can put some numbers together, and we can go from there." He opened a long drawer under the bookcase, and Christie saw more rolls of plans. He added the plan they'd been reviewing, then closed the drawer.

"Thanks. I can't see selling, though, if Curtis doesn't sell part of his land. It would bring the subdivision too close to our home."

"Don't worry about that. It's all taken care of."

Chapter Eight

After Christie left the Webster office, she felt like she needed a shower. She hated lying, but she had to find out what they had planned, and it was as they'd feared. The boys were in the process of trying to get Curtis declared incompetent. They had to stop it, but how should they proceed? She pulled up to Orchid's house to see that the front door was now a bright orange.

A quirky house for a quirky lady.

As she exited the truck, she decided to take a quick stopover at the Matthews home. Kurt's wife had been pretty upset before, but she wanted to make sure that things had calmed down since their last conversation. Christie tapped on the door, mindful that the younger children may be napping. The door opened, and Carole stood in front of her, the evidence of grief had aged her.

"Hello. I wanted to come by and see if you all needed anything. I'd be happy to go to the store, or if you need any chores done, I can help with that."

Carole's eyes filled with tears, and she pulled a used tissue from her pocket. She wiped her eyes. "You're sweet for asking. Right now, what we need is justice."

"I understand."

"No, you don't," she squeaked. "Why do people say they understand? They don't understand. Someone I love has been taken from me. I won't rest until whoever did this pays for what they did."

"We don't know—"

"Oh, yes, we do. Curtis Altgelt killed my husband. And he's going to jail."

"But—"

"But nothing. We got the report. The bullet that killed Kurt came from Curtis's gun. He's going to be arrested, if he hasn't been already."

Christie took a step back. "What?"

"Yes, that's right. He did it. I told you he did. Now, I don't want to be rude, but please leave." Mrs. Matthews shut the door.

Stunned by the conversation, Christie called her father's phone. It went straight to voicemail. She tried Curtis's phone but received the same response. She looked up to see Orchid standing at the entrance. The woman waved at Christie, who made her way across the street and up to the door.

"What is it, child? You look like you've seen a ghost. Come inside."

Christie followed her to the kitchen where Orchid poured hot water into a cup and added a chamomile tea bag. "Here. Now tell me what's going on."

Christie shared about her time at the realty company and her conversation with Mrs. Matthews. "I'm worried. Neither Pop nor Curtis picked up their phone."

"Worrying will not change a dot. You call back in a minute." She sipped at her tea.

"I feel so helpless. That's all."

"We all feel that way at times. But you're not helpless. You don't know what you don't know, and when you know, then you'll know what to do."

"Huh?" Christie grinned at Orchid.

"See, better already." Orchid untied a multi-colored scarf with leaves around her neck. "Do we want to reschedule our trip to San Antonio?"

“I’m not sure.” Christie cupped the porcelain mug in her hand, allowing the warmth to penetrate her skin.

“Well, I’m sure. You will be thinking about this instead of enjoying our day, so let’s work on getting this resolved, and we can save the trip for another day.”

“Okay, thanks. I think you’re right.” Christie took another sip and allowed it to calm her frazzled nerves. “I’m going to try calling again.” She dialed in the number for Pop’s phone. This time, he answered, and she put the phone on speaker. “Pop, are you and Curtis okay? I tried calling but got no answer.”

“Depends on how you determine fine. That whippersnapper, Hug, came and carted Curtis off to jail. Can you believe it?”

“Pop, he’s Sheriff Clauson now. You can’t call him Hug.”

“I sure can. He’ll always be that scrawny little boy to me.”

“Fine. But what happened?”

“We were sitting in the house, and Hug came and

said that ballistics showed that the bullet that killed Kurt Matthews came from Curtis's gun. I told him there was no way Curtis killed him."

"But Curtis took a shot at the scarecrow? He said so himself."

"I'm telling ya, Curtis didn't kill anyone."

"Pop, do you think–I'm just thinking out loud here–that Curtis accidently shot Kurt when he came home that night and tried to cover it up by saying he shot Kurt after he returned?"

"No way. I'd swear to that on your mother's Bible."

"You can swear to believe him, Pop, but it is a possibility, and we have to consider it."

"No. I'll not consider anything that has my friend shooting someone on purpose or even, accidently. He didn't do it."

"Okay. What happens now?"

"They hauled him off in handcuffs. Handcuffs! Can you believe it?" Pop spat through the phone. "Christie, he said that he wants you to come see him tomorrow."

"Okay, I can do that."

He blew out a breath. "What happened with the

vultures?"

"I told them about selling our property but wanted to ensure Curtis would also sell a portion of his land. They told me not to worry about it; that it was all taken care of."

"See? That's proof, right there."

"Pop, proof of what exactly?"

"They're trying to get Curtis out of the picture. And you know who has the most to gain from it."

"Yes, Erik and Nick. But we can't prove that either of them killed Kurt."

"Think about it, Christie. They discover Curtis has a son. He's the rightful heir, and he can cause all kinds of problems for them. They find out he's going to meet Curtis, and they kill him."

"Okay, Pop. But how would they find that out? Kurt had told no one. At least that we know." Something niggled at the back of her mind. "Pop, I have an idea I want to check out. Please go to the house and stay put. I'll be home later. Orchid and I are putting off our trip to San Antonio until another day.

"Okay. But we have to help Curtis."

"We will. See you later."

Christie ended the call. She looked at Orchid who spoke. "I have to agree with your father. Something is awfully fishy going on."

"Agreed, but our hands are tied. However, to be honest, I'm almost thankful Curtis is in jail. At least there, he'll be safe from whoever is causing all this havoc."

Orchid pulled on her earlobe. "What's your idea?"

"My idea?"

"You told your father you had an idea to help Curtis. I'm already dressed, so let's get to it."

"Oh, yeah. I'm wondering if Kurt left anything that showed a connection to Curtis. I would think if there's anything like that, it would be in his truck or his office. Unfortunately, the Websters are super quick to clean things. I do wonder, though." She took a sip of the tea. "Hold on. I'll be right back." She hopped up and went out the front door. The car was no longer in the drive, but a minivan sat in the driveway. Christie knocked on the door and waited. A minute later, the door cracked open, and it was Kurt's daughter, Lana. She opened the door wider at seeing Christie. “Hi. Hey, heard you earlier with Mom. I hope you’ll forgive her. She’s not really herself right now.”

“No need to apologize. It’s a terrible tragedy.”

“Yes, we were all so excited to come out here. Now, Mom’s already talking about moving back home. I just registered the kids in school. The thought of taking them out again...” She looked down at the shabby stuffed bunny in her hands. “I don’t feel I can do that to them, but I’m not sure what we’ll do now.”

“I was serious when I told your mom about whatever you all need. Please let me help.”

“Okay. I’ll remember that. Now, what can I help you with?”

“Listen, by any chance, did they give you a box of your dad’s stuff from his office?”

“I think so. Come in, and I’ll see.” She left Christie in the living room and came back carrying a banker’s box. “Yes, here it is.”

“Do you think I could borrow it for a bit?”

Lana cocked her head and was silent for a minute. “I guess. But I’ll need it back before my mom comes home. She wouldn't be happy I gave it to anyone."

"I'm just going to take it across the street and look through it. Shouldn't take long at all. When's your mom coming back?"

"She went into San Antonio to Fort Sam cemetery. My dad served, and he'll be buried there." Her face grew blotchy and red, and tears spilled down her cheeks. "He was a good man. I don't know why anyone would want to harm him."

"Unfortunately, bad people don't care if a person's good. They only care about themselves."

"Here, if you can have this back in, say, an hour or two?" She handed the box to Christie.

"I'll have it back shortly. Thanks. It may not contain anything important, but I want justice for your dad, too. We just have to make sure the right person goes to jail."

She nodded and closed the door. Christie felt the lightness of the box and realized it may not help at all, but better to check for any leads.

Inside Orchid's house, they opened the box. Inside were standard desk items: a desk name plate, framed real estate certificates, business cards from individuals, a calendar with dates and times of meetings, but nothing that showed his meeting with Curtis. Lastly, it contained a couple of legal pads. One of them had writing on the front with to-do's on gathering zoning information and another one was more personal items, like, pick up dry-cleaning and other tasks. Other than a few books that held nothing important, there wasn't anything out of the ordinary.

Christie huffed. "Shoot. That was a dead-end. But at least we can mark it off."

"Wait, a minute." Orchid picked up the legal pad with the to-do list on top. Items were scratched off, and others were written in bullet form that would never be completed. "Look at this. She showed a crease at the top."

"Sorry?"

"This is when you want to write something down but keep the main items on top. He used pages underneath. Look." She turned the sheet over and watched as Orchid showed strips of pages that had been torn out.

"Too bad we don't know what the pages contained. A dead-end."

"Maybe not." Orchid rose and went to a drawer where she pulled out a sharpened pencil. She started moving the pencil back and forth across the page.

While some letters were lighter because of the pressure, one word stood out.

Father?

The other words led to them filling in with the letters—*Curtis Altgelt*.

Who had seen this?

"If he kept this in his office, anyone at Webster Realty could have seen it. But I'm not sure how that helps, unless they said something to Erik or Nick."

Orchid sat back in her chair. "If it meant that it could cause problems for them, I'm sure they'd say something about it to them or confront Kurt about it. If only we knew if that ever happened."

"I wonder."

"Yes?" Orchid leaned on the table and waited.

"Today, when I went to the office, I met their receptionist, Lisa. She would know who comes and goes, and I'm sure she's overheard things, too. Maybe I should have a chat with her."

"I think I should go. I can say he'd been talking to me about a possible purchase. But I think we should arrive separately."

"Okay. But what should I say?"

"Didn't you say they had pictures of houses in the conference room? Once I arrive and keep her occupied, then you can go in there and do some snooping in the drawers. Maybe it will give us another clue. But we need to make sure the Websters aren't there."

"I'm beginning to think you're getting into this too much." She winked at Orchid.

"It's something different, and you know how I like different."

"They were headed out to another appointment so we should be good. Let me run this box back over to the Matthews first."

Christie returned the box, then headed to Webster Realty. She arrived to see Lisa chatting on the phone. The young woman raised a finger to wait before signing off.

"Hello, again. I'm sorry, but the Websters are out of the office right now."

"I'm actually here to see if I can peek at the pictures of the houses and blueprints. I wanted to do it earlier and forgot when I left. Is that okay?"

"Certainly. Be happy to show you."

"Oh, I can go myself."

"We have to accompany clients in there. Just let me get my headphones—"

The door to the office opened, and Orchid entered. She wore a styled wig, a massive diamond ring on her right hand, a braided gold chain, and a large bag with the iconic L's and V's on it. She'd changed into a couture Chanel outfit, and the transformation was astonishing. She had expertly applied makeup and the transformation was remarkable. Christie struggled not to gape. Orchid breezed into the room with nary a glance at Christie.

"Hello." She'd changed her natural tone, and the accent was upper class. "I'd like to speak to the owner, please." She smiled at the stymied Lisa.

"Hello. I'm Lisa." She rose and wiped her hands on her skirt before extending it to Orchid.

Orchid looked at Lisa's hand and touched her fingers lightly. "Charmed, I'm sure."

Christie rolled her eyes.

Wow, Orchid is good.

"I'm from New Orleans, and I am considering a move to the area. Someone recommended I contact this firm. I'm sure it's the best?" She looked around as if determining the worthiness of the institution and her time.

Lisa's head bobbed up and down in symbolic agreement. "Yes, ma'am. It is. I know they would love to meet you. I, um, they're not here right now, but I can call them. Or, if you prefer, I could set up an appointment." As Lisa scurried behind her desk, Orchid motioned with her head.

Christie had been so caught up in this new persona, she'd forgotten her mission. "Lisa, I'm going to pop in and look at the house pictures."

"Um, well, okay." It was evident who held the power in this situation, and she was determined to impress the wealthy person standing in front of her versus the local gal. Christie made sure Orchid was keeping Lisa busy while she went down the hall. She heard a voice talking behind a door. She assumed Albert was talking on the phone to a client. She looked at the office doors, but they were all closed. No way she'd know which had been Kurt's.

She entered the conference room and looked around. Not much she could find out here. Then, her gaze went to the bookcase with the large drawers next to it, from where Tyler had returned the map. Listening for a minute, she heard Orchid carrying on about her requirements for a home. Christie closed the door to the conference room and quickly made her way to the drawers. Looking up, she noticed the carved owl she'd seen earlier. The top left ear bore the marks of a fall and what appeared to be a lame attempt at fixing the coloring. It was a unique piece with its large eyes and puffy plumage. She drew in closer and could see the patina on its wings.

Must be an antique. Beautiful.

She pulled open the drawer where Tyler had

replaced the map. Next to it was a rolled-up parcel with a question mark and "Estates" written on it. Listening for a minute, Christie pulled out the parcel and opened it. It showed a subdivision with houses on a half-acre to one-acre plots. Hundreds of them. She looked at the bottom and saw "Phase One." Out from the main road area, they had drawn a gated area in and behind it, the words "Phase Two."

Phase One! Their plan was to develop the entire area into high-end lots and homes. She opened the page and saw a schematic showing a few house facades. The diagram showed the homes starting at seven-hundred thousand for the smaller models. No wonder the Websters were so adamant about getting their hands on the two properties. They stood to make millions. What they would pay for their property and Curtis's was a drop in the bucket compared to what they'd sell the lots for, in addition to building the homes. She rolled it up and put it back in the drawer.

Five acre lots my foot.

A picture of a home's interior on the wall caught her head. She craned her head to get a better look it when the door opened, and Albert came in.

His eyes widened and he halted his approach. “Sorry, didn’t know you were in here. Are you waiting for someone?” He stuck his head in the hall toward the reception area. Lisa could be heard trying to set an appointment time with Orchid.

“No, just admiring the houses. I came in earlier and met with the Websters, and I meant to inspect these and the blueprints. I’m considering having a house built, but maybe something smaller.”

“We will build some townhomes that run around thirty-five thousand square feet. No maintenance, as we will include it with the HOA.”

“That sounds nice. Can you show me something?”

He hesitated. “It’s all still in the planning stages, but I’d be happy to share them with you later. We’re still looking for the perfect property for it. Did I see you speaking with the Websters earlier?”

“Yes. We’re looking into possibly doing some business together.” An idea came to her. “I’d been speaking with Kurt, but he wasn’t able to help me too much. He said he didn’t have all the information since he was new on the job, but he said he would be happy to connect me with the Websters. Then, he was killed."

"Yes, really sad. Kurt said nothing about the subdivision?"

"Subdivision?" Christie played dumb.

"It's a new project that's been talked about. We've had some interest with a silent partner, and it may help move the project forward faster."

"Oh, that sounds exciting. I must tell you that living in my father's place leaves a bit to be desired. If something would break ground soon, that would be great."

Albert moved away from the door and toward the conference table. "It's probably best you speak to the Websters, and they can answer all your questions."

"What can I help with?" Tyler spoke from the door causing Christie to jump.

"Oh, hello again. You startled me." Christie laughed.

"Did you need something else, or has Albert helped you?" He showed his straight white teeth in a haphazard attempt at a smile.

"She said she had been speaking with Kurt."

Tyler moved inside the room. "You'd been speaking to Kurt? What about?"

"He wanted to share about some properties in town that were available when he heard I was staying at my father's for now. I told him I would be building on the property, and he told me you all have some wonderful home plans. That's partly why I came this morning. I forgot to take a closer look at these." She pointed to the photos once she realized she was rambling.

"Okay. Again, we're delighted to work with you on any project. Please let us know if we can be of any future assistance. Unfortunately, we have a client coming in, and we're preparing to meet with them. Lisa can help you set up another time to look over the various plans we offer." With a dismissive wave, he ushered her out the door.

Outside of the establishment, Christie took a deep breath. Had she made things worse with her visit? She turned and waved at Tyler, who stood inside the office, staring at her through the window.

She climbed into her truck and headed down Main

Street. Orchid was nowhere in sight. Her mind raced.

If Kurt knew about the subdivision planning, had that been what he'd wanted to tell Curtis that evening? Christie needed to find out exactly what Kurt and Curtis had shared the night Kurt was killed.

Chapter Nine

By the time Christie arrived home, horse trailers were unloading more horses into the second paddock area. She parked her truck and headed out to the activity.

"Hey, Pop. I didn't realize that Curtis had so many horses." She noticed an old mare being carefully walked down the trailer ramp.

"Well, not all of these are his. Some of these are older, but they aren't in any pain. Curtis told the vet he would take any horse like that and let it live out its last days on his property."

"That's so sweet. But how did he plan to manage that? There's no way he could care for all these horses on his own." Christie reached up and stroked the mare's muzzle before she was led away.

"I hear ya. The vet says they'll help out when they can, and Curtis has an idea. In fact, his lawyer will be here soon to talk to us."

Christie crossed her arms. "His lawyer? Why would

he be coming here to see us?"

"You'll see soon enough, darling." He took off his hat and wiped his forehead before replacing it. "Need to help get these all finished before he gets here."

"Okay, let me go change, and I can help."

"Naw, we got it. Plus, he should be here shortly. Also, we found that insurance. Sure nuff, he had coverage for his barn. So that means we can build a brand new one, bigger and better." He waved her off and took up the reins of another horse just off a trailer, leading it gently toward the stables.

~~~

Christie headed toward the house but the word "we" kept echoing in her mind. What did Pop mean by that, or had he simply misspoken?

Within a short amount of time, the horses were all settled in stalls or paddocks. Everyone left, and Pop went in to change out of his work clothing. Christie heard a car approaching and looked out to see a brand-new Cadillac Escalade pull up next to her truck. A gentleman in a gray suit and polished black shoes
~~~

exited the automobile. He pulled out a handkerchief and wiped his face and bald head, before putting it back in his pocket and reaching in to retrieve a briefcase from inside the vehicle. From the passenger door, a young Hispanic woman exited, carrying a large navy bag.

Christie held open the screen door. "Hello. I'm Christie Taylor."

The man walked up the steps onto the porch and shook her hand. "Nice to meet you, Miss Taylor. I'm Ronald Manet. This is Beatrice Salazar."

"Mr. Manet, Ms. Salazar, please come in." She ushered them inside the house.

"Call me Ron. No need for the formality." He adjusted the polished leather briefcase with his initials embossed in gold on the side. "Are we ready to proceed?"

"I'm sorry, but I'm not sure—"

Pop entered the room, his hair wet from the shower he'd taken. "Hello, there. You must be Ronnie. Ronald and Carrie's son."

"Yes, sir. They go way back with Mr. Altgelt. I

believe he helped them out when they had some issues back during the recession in the seventies."

Pop clapped the man on the back. "Only what neighbors do. Now, let's go have a sit at the table, shall we? Ma'am." He shook the woman's hand.

Christie followed the group, her mind racing as to what the lawyer's presence meant. In the kitchen, Ron opened his briefcase and pulled out a series of documents. "Miss Taylor, these documents contain power of attorney giving you full rights over everything concerning Curtis Altgelt's various concerns. By signing each of these documents, you agree to be the sole authority to act on the behalf of Mr. Altgelt, should he be unable to handle his affairs. This power of attorney supplies you with broad legal authority, should you be required to make legal decisions about Mr. Altgelt's property, finances, or medical care. Do you understand this responsibility as I have explained it to you?"

Christie took the papers handed to her and read the pages of legalese. "Pop, what is this, and why has Curtis named me?"

"You know as well as I do that people are out to destroy Curtis and get his land. He needs someone to have his back. Curtis wants someone that will follow his wishes, and who else better than you for that. He also knows his health is declining, so that's why he wants to set up the property to be used in perpetuity as an equine rescue and hospice. By doing this, those boys won't be able to say he needs to hand over authority to them as he's already given it to you. Should they proceed with guardianship, he's already included you as guardian as well."

"But—"

Ron picked up another set of papers. "Are you saying you wish to decline this offer, Miss Taylor?"

"No. I'm just shocked, that's all." She looked at the documents in his hand. "Is there anything else?"

"Yes. He's also made you executor of his will. He has made provisions for compensating you for that position, as you can see here."

Christie plopped down into a chair as Ronald set the other set of papers in front of her. "This is too much. I think I should speak with Curtis first."

“He said you would say that, and so here’s a letter he wrote to you.” Ron pulled a sealed envelope with her name on it from a pocket inside his briefcase.

Christie opened the letter and read Curtis’s note.

“Please sign the documents. You’re the only one who can stop them.”

“Can I think about it?” Christie set the letter down and gazed up at him.

Ron pulled another letter from his satchel with her name on it. “He thought of everything.”

“No time to waste, as the vultures are already circling.”

Christie chuckled. “I guess I’ve met my match. Where do I need to sign?”

“If you don’t mind, I’d like you to read the documents in full, please initial each page here and here,” he pointed at the places on the documents, “and sign your legal name here.”

A sound came from Beatrice’s phone. “Sorry, I have a closing after this.” She muted the phone and returned it to her purse. Beatrice pulled out a large pad and a stamp. She asked for Christie’s identification.

After Christie had signed the various documents, the woman notarized the signing of the official papers and put her items away.

"Nice to meet you." She shook hands with Christie and Pop.

"Nice to meet you, too." Christie stood. "What happens next?"

Ron secured the pages into the briefcase. "I'll be making copies of all of these and will return them to you at that point. I will also let Mr. Altgelt know we have completed this matter." He pulled a heavy cream business card from an inside pocket. "Should you have questions, please call me at this number."

After the pair drove off, Christie said, "Pop, you have a lot of explaining to do. You should have given me a heads-up."

"Would've, Christie, but Curtis wanted to keep it on the down-low. If anyone got wind that he was giving you power of attorney and guardianship where the land couldn't be sold without your permission, they could have caused problems."

A thought raced through Christie's mind. She

yelled, "Yep, Pop. He's effectively put a target on my back!"

"Settle down now. Unless them boys try something, no one's to know."

She sighed. "I guess you're right but this whole business makes me nervous as all get-out. Now, I'm going to change, and we can make sure all the horses are good for the night." She looked around. "By the way, where's Mutt and Jeffrey?" It had just occurred to her that the two labs were missing from their usual spots.

"I took them over to Curtis's for a while. It can help spook off animals when they hear dogs barking, and the boys can lay down their scent in case any critters come back to mess with his chickens. But you know them. They took off after something in the bushes. I expect they'll be home in a while when it'll be getting close to supper."

Something niggled at Christie's mind. "Just a minute, Pop." Christie jogged back into the kitchen where the lawyer's business card sat on the table. She entered the number on her phone. "I'm sorry to bother you, but I have a question."

"Yes, how can I assist you?" Ron replied.

"The lady that came with you. She said she was going to a closing after meeting with us."

"That's right. She does the notarization for a local firm when they have closings. Sorry, I just dropped her off if you needed to speak with her. Why?"

"Can you tell me who that is?" Christie waited for the answer.

"I don't see why not. It's Webster Development."

Christie groaned. "Thank you."

"Is everything okay?" Ron responded.

"Yes, thank you." She set the phone down and put her head in her hands. If Beatrice did all their closings, would she say anything to the Websters? Someone could easily see Christie's signature if they were signing on the same page in the notary's book. It may have been that no one would know about it, but now, she couldn't count on it not getting back to the Websters. If the Websters knew, she was sure they'd tell Erik and Nick. A shiver ran up her spine. Whoever had made sure Kurt was out of the way wouldn't stop to do the same to her. For the first time in her life, Christie was truly afraid.

Chapter Ten

"Orchid, I still owe you a day out on the Riverwalk. Are you up for an outing tomorrow? I think I need to get out of Dodge for a bit."

"That doesn't sound good, but I would love to take you up on the offer. What time tomorrow?"

"Say around nine or ten?" Christie shifted the phone to her other ear.

"Wonderful. Let's do nine, so we can stop at the museum on the way and eat lunch on the Riverwalk afterward. Does that sound okay?"

"Yep. Works for me. See you tomorrow." Christie signed off the call. Pop had gone to visit with Curtis, so Christie tackled some cleaning chores. She cranked up the music and sang along as she cleaned and dusted. Since the house was compact, she made quick work of the job. She decided to take Champ out for a short ride. After saddling him up, she took the verge along the road leading to the Altgelt ranch. The sun was warm on her back, and she lavished in its ability to calm her jangled nerves.

Arriving at the Curtis homestead, she walked Champ up the drive but was shocked to see two vehicles there. But that wasn't what caused her to suck in a breath. Erik and Beatrice were locked in an embrace.

Great. No denying who knew about her having power of attorney or becoming executor now. She didn't think she could leave without them seeing her, so she backed up Champ further behind a hedge of trees and cleared her throat while speaking loudly. "Champ, are you getting thirsty, boy?"

She stayed for a minute longer, then moved around the tree to see that Erik and Beatrice now faced her. "Oh, hello. I didn't know Curtis was expecting anyone."

Erik took a step toward her. "I came out to see if he'd been released from jail yet. I see he's not here, so I guess I'll go there and find out what's happening."

Christie halted Champ. "Miss Salazar, is it?"

The woman straightened her jacket and tossed her

shiny, ebony hair over her shoulder. "Yes." She turned to Erik. "Well, Mr. Stewart, nice meeting you. Again, if you need any further notary work, please contact me." She shoved on a pair of sunglasses before entering her Lexus.

Christie backed Champ away from the road and watched as the woman drove away. She needed to convince Curtis to put in a gate. Turning back to Erik, she decided it was better to be direct. "I've heard that you had considered some legal pursuit against Curtis. I believe we both know you no longer need to do anything like that."

She watched as he struggled between acting like he didn't know or admitting Beatrice had told him. "I don't know what you mean. Nick and I only want what's best for the old man."

"By trying to steal his land and home out from under him?"

He shielded his eyes. "Who's playing games now? I also heard you may be looking into selling some of the Taylor ranch, too."

Christie should have realized that would have

gotten back to them. “I’m just looking into options.”

Erik sneered. “Good to have control of this property and able to convince your father. You should do all right, I’d say. But let’s come to some better terms. I think that we can come up with a plan that will benefit all of us.”

Christie stroked Champ’s neck. “I’m listening.”

“I think we could all get what we want if we work together.”

“Okay, but what about Curtis? He needs to be cleared of Kurt’s murder.” She motioned for Erik to follow her over to the water trough so Champ could drink.

“My hands are tied on that. I don’t understand why Curtis did what he did. I think he’s senile or something. Kurt just got in the way.”

“Being murdered is not ‘getting in the way.’” She huffed. “Did you know that Kurt was Curtis’s son?”

Erik took a step back. “What? Who told you that?”

He was a good actor, or he truly didn’t know about the connection. “So, you didn’t know Kurt Matthews was Curtis’s son?”

"How would I know that? I always thought he couldn't have kids." He shook his head. "I didn't know. I wonder why Curtis killed him, then?"

Christie patted Champ on his neck. "He didn't. Someone else did. Someone who had a motive to kill him."

Erik bristled. "Are you accusing me of murder?"

"I'm simply saying someone wanted Kurt dead, and Curtis to take the blame. There aren't too many people—"

"Wait. Are you saying that Nick could have killed him to frame Curtis?"

"Again, I'm not saying anything. I'm simply asking a question."

Erik turned and moved over to a stump. He wiped it off and sat. He shook his head. "I know Nick is having some business concerns, but I can't see him doing something like that."

"Business concerns?" Christie led Champ to a spot of shade.

"His business is struggling. He needs a hit of cash flow, and soon. I offered to give him some money to tide him over, but he refused. Said he'd work it out. I know he wanted to get some of the property sold because that would give him enough to make up for his losses and provide assets for next year."

"Nick has a motive, then," Christie spoke before regretting saying it aloud.

Erik rose and dusted off his pants. "I guess you could say we all have motive. Even you." He pointed his finger at her.

"Me? What possible motive do I have?"

"Oh, I don't know. Let's think about this." He ticked off with his fingers. "You move back, and Curtis is seriously hurt and almost killed in an accident in an area you told him about. Two, you've talked with the Websters about selling some of your property conveniently next to this place, and three, you now have guardianship." He leaned toward her. "That's a lot of motive, lady."

Christie laughed. "We saved his life. Plus, I didn't ask to have power—and who told you that—Beatrice? Isn't that against the law?"

"She didn't tell me. I was at a closing the other day.

Bought some investment property on Main Street in Boerne. I saw your name there. Plus, the attorney told us since Curtis wanted us to know."

"Who was at the closing?"

His face scrunched up before he responded. "Why?"

"Just curious." She stroked Champ's neck.

"Um, let's see. Me of course. Nick, as he's my partner on it. Tyler, Albert, Beatrice, and I think Emma came in for a bit."

Apparently, Nick and Tyler had both seen that she had signed the documents. Erik could easily act like he didn't know anything. All three stood to make a ton of money, once they could develop the properties. Even Albert and Emma had a stake in getting the properties. But what motive would they have for killing Kurt? Who had torn out the page in Kurt's book about his relationship with his father? But if Nick had major financial problems, Kurt coming into the picture would have caused serious delays if not outright stopping of the project moving forward.

She swung herself up on Champ's back. "I need to

get back to the house. By the way, where were you and Nick the night of Kurt's death?"

"You playing detective now? I don't have to answer your questions, but just so you'll stop worrying your pretty little mind about it, I was on a business trip. I can't tell you where Nick was during that time. All I know is that he was 'out-of-pocket' at some camp."

"Camp?" Christie turned Champ toward the road.

"Yep, he went camping and shooting that week."

On the ride home, Christie's mind went over their conversation. Nick had financial troubles, he knew how to shoot, and he had plenty of motive to see Curtis deemed incompetent or in jail. Plus, with Kurt out of the way, he probably thought he'd fixed that problem. The only thing was that Kurt had already spoken to Curtis about being his son, so he couldn't control that now. It would stand to reason that Kurt's family would inherit anything due to him. But what nagged at Christie was that Kurt had wanted to tell Curtis something important. From what Curtis had said, Kurt hadn't divulged anything other than Curtis's parentage. They were going to meet up again, but it never happened. Could that have been about the subdivision, or had it been something else entirely? They'd never know now.

~~~

Riding back to the house, Christie took her time ensuring that Champ was cared for before releasing him in the paddock. A ding on her phone let her know someone was at the gate. She looked at the video. It was Jess and his dad, Mike. She opened the gate for them.

Christie walked around to the front and watched as the dually pickup made its way down the drive. Behind it, they pulled a smaller travel trailer. Christie waved as the truck pulled over and stopped in front of a post. Jess swung out of his side, already having grown an inch since she had last seen him. "Hey, Jess. Good to see you."

"Hello, Miss Taylor. I thought I'd come out for a bit and help out with the horses."

"Thanks. We can sure use the help. If you'll start work on the back stalls, I can assist you in a little
~~~

while."

"Got it." The lanky teenager headed toward the stables.

Mike exited the truck. He was stocky, and his reddened neck and face showed the time he spent outdoors. His rough hand borne from manual labor enveloped hers. "Howdy there. I've been meaning to stop by and thank y'all for allowing Jess to stay here for the rest of the school year. I've taken off as much time as I can, and I'll have to head back to Midland soon."

"No problem. We're happy we can help. You really didn't need to buy a travel trailer though. We could have worked it out."

"I know you'll be building a house out here soon, but I also know how moody teens can be. This way, hopefully, everyone has some space and don't end up killing one another." He burst out in a deep, melodious laugh.

"Well, thanks. Would you like to come in for some iced tea, or do you need to leave soon?"

He nodded. "I never turn down an invitation for

tea. Don't suppose you have any pie to go with it?"

"Are bluebonnets the Texas state flower?" She grinned.

"Great." He rubbed his hands together. "I hoped you'd say that. Been hearing about how good your pies are, and I have been wanting to try one."

"Should we call Jess?"

"Nah. Let him work while he's in the mood. That's what I always say. He can come in later." He motioned for her to go in front of him.

Inside the kitchen, Christie poured tea and cut a slice of caramel apple pie for Mike. "Here you go." She handed him a fork.

"Thank ya kindly, ma'am. As you can imagine, we don't get a lot of good home-cooking out in the oil fields." He took a big bite and chewed. "Um, um. That is some good pie. It's all in the crust. Right?"

"That's what I say." Christie took a sip of the tea.

In a minute, Mike sat back. He sighed. "That was mighty tasty. Thanks."

"Mike, I'm sorry—"

"I bet I know what you're going to say. You know,

it's funny. You would have thought I would have seen the signs. But we're divorced now, and it's just me and Jess. We'll make it. I try to talk to Jess about his mother, but he doesn't want to talk about her. I don't know if he ever will."

"Give him time. Even when someone is still alive, but is out of your life, it's a time of grieving." She poured more tea into their glasses.

"Yep. I've been doing that myself. It's been months, but it feels raw some days." He laughed. "Guys are already after me to start dating, but that's the last thing on my mind. For now, I've got to focus on me and Jess."

"That's smart. I think it will do you good. And listen, you're more than welcome to come here on the weekends and hang out with Jess. Just be forewarned, we may put you to work."

"I'm good with that, if I can trade it for some good meals." He grinned. "Well, best be unloading that trailer. How about showing me where it should go?"

After they'd maneuvered the trailer close to the house where they could hook up the electrical and access to water, they found Jess in the barn. He was almost finished with the stalls.

"Wow, you're a hard worker, Jess. I don't see anything left to do." Christie smiled, and Jess beamed at the praise. "There's pie in the house if you want some."

After he headed to the house, Mike looked around. "Y'all have your hands full with all these horses."

"They're some of Curtis's and some from the local vet. And of course, you remember this guy." She led him over to Champ, who nodded his head up and down in agreement and recognition.

"Hey, there, boy. So good to see you have a nice, new owner." Mike patted the horse.

"I best be heading back. Let me get the boy." Mike and Jess climbed back in the truck.

Christie walked around to the passenger side where Mike sat. "Thanks for stopping by."

"Thank you." He gripped her hand in his beefy one. A surge of electricity went down her arm. Their eyes met for a moment.

Static electricity. That's what it was.

Christie waved as the pair drove away.

Chapter Eleven

The following morning, Christie and Orchid headed into San Antonio. The weather held, and the day was comfortable. After a stop at the McNay Art Museum, they ate at The Guenther House, where they enjoyed a lunch of chicken salad. They finished the time with a stroll on the path next to the San Antonio River. Orchid opened an umbrella with parrots across the fabric. . Its colors matched the vibrant dress she wore.

Christie brought Orchid up to speed on what had been happening, and Orchid listened intently. "That doesn't sound good. I want you to be extra vigilant now. I don't want anything happening to my new friend."

"Me either!" Christie laughed.

"What's your opinion on what Erik said? Do you think he was being honest, or was he trying to put the blame on Nick?"

"I wasn't there, sweetie, so I have no way to know,

but it sounds like this Nick has plenty of motive and plenty of opportunity. Do you know where he was camping?"

"No. So that's a dead end. I guess I'll have to figure out some way to find out."

"I'd be careful. If someone is that desperate, they're going to try again."

Even with the warm sun on her back, Christie shivered. "I know. I've said as much. Plus, with Jess going to be living with us, I don't want anything to happen to him, either. Thankfully, I convinced Pop to put in the gate, so that's stopped many people coming and going without our knowledge."

"True." Orchid shifted the umbrella to her other hand, the bangles on her arm jingling together. "However, it doesn't mean they'll come after you only on your land. It could be anywhere. Again, extra vigilant my friend." She lowered her head and stared at Christie.

"Cross my heart." Christie said and motioned with her fingers. "I will."

"Good. Now where are we going for dessert?"

"I don't know. Any ideas?"

"You know what I miss?"

"What?" Christie moved over as a person on a bike rode past.

"Bambino Huey's."

"Oh, I used to love those growing up. Unfortunately, they don't make them anymore. They had them in the freezer section at HEB for a while. But no more."

"Time marches on." Orchid sighed.

"True," Christie agreed. "So, any thoughts on where we could go?"

"I know. How about Dough? I love their polenta cake."

"Sounds good. We could get the sampler and split it." Christie turned toward the parking lot.

"Even better." Orchid closed her umbrella as they got into the car.

After enjoying the dessert and coffee, Christie dropped Orchid off at her house and drove home. She contemplated how age never mattered when kindred spirits connected. She was happy that, as different as they were in age and personality, she'd made a great new friend in Orchid.

Christie sang along to the music in her truck's stereo system as she drove home. By the time she made it to the gate, she saw lights headed up the road toward Curtis's place.

Probably some kids out joyriding.

She opened the gate and drove on through to the house. Lights were on, and she greeted Pop and Jess, who were watching a show on television. That night she slept better than she had in months, but her phone ringing woke her early.

The ringing stopped.

Must have been a spam call. No voicemail.

Christie threw back the covers and sat on the side of the bed. As the mental fog cleared, she reached over and grabbed her new robe. Shoving her feet into slippers, she shuffled to the kitchen. Pouring a cup of coffee, she tried to figure out her next steps. Christie pulled the phone from her pocket and looked at the number again. She didn't recognize it.

Opening the back door, she spied Pop already out

by the barns. He waved at her before picking up the handles of a wheelbarrow with a hay bale in it. Even at his age, and now with a bum shoulder, the work kept him busy and happy.

After the coffee had its desired effect, she looked up to see Pop on the back porch. He scraped his boots on the metal bar next to the door and entered. "Morning Pop. Want me to make some breakfast?"

"Nah. I'm good. Not right now. I need to get over to Curtis's place and check on the chickens and water his garden."

Christie noted his tired face. "Why don't I do that, and you sit down and rest for a bit? Looks like you've been hard at work. What time did you get up?"

"Bit before five. Can't sleep knowing Curtis is in that place, and by of no fault of his own."

Christie poured coffee into a mug and set it in front of her father. "I know. It's frustrating that our hands are tied. But I was more worried about him being alone over there with a killer on the loose."

He took a sip of the coffee. "Yep. There is that. But Hug ain't doing nothing."

"Pop, he has to wait for evidence from the medical examiner and others. Once they find something that shows Curtis couldn't have killed Kurt, they'll let him go." She stood and rinsed her cup in the sink, then hung it from a hook to dry. "In fact, I've been given some information I'm going to take to the sheriff today."

"Oh, yeah? From who?"

"Believe it or not, from Erik. He gave me some details about Nick's finances that may interest the sheriff."

"Or more likely, he's trying to point the finger at Nick so none of the suspicion falls on him." Coffee sloshed over the side of Pop's cup and he wiped it up with a napkin.

"That may be true, but all I can do is share with the sheriff and let him see if it's worth pursuing." She hugged Pop's neck. "I'm going to get dressed, then I'll head over to Curtis's.

It wasn't long before Christie found herself on the road toward Curtis's house. She parked her truck and walked toward the back. As she rounded the corner, a silver Mercedes faced her. Nick's car.

"Of all the—" Christie glanced around but didn't see him.

She approached the car, and as she did, the hair on her arms stood on end. Nick was slumped over on the front seat. His face was an odd shade of grey-blue with a red tinge to it. Christie jogged to the back of the vehicle. Someone had blocked the exhaust. She whipped out her phone and called 911.

After reporting her location, she went around the car and looked in the passenger side window. On the floorboard, a piece of legal paper lie face up. It looked familiar, and Christie realized it was the paper Kurt had written. Under it, in block letters, she read the words, "I did it." She stepped back from the car.

Had Nick killed Kurt and decided he couldn't live with himself?

She cupped her hands and looked back into the car. She wanted so badly to open the door, but she knew she would destroy vital evidence. But evidence of what—suicide or a murder made to look like suicide? She scanned the floor and saw a bottle of what appeared to be whiskey. So, had Nick driven out here, meaning to take his own life? It wouldn't be long before the sheriff and deputies arrived. She jogged over to the garden and started up the water spigot. She then went over to the chicken coop and checked the scratch and water. All the chickens were fine; no signs of any raccoons or fox trying to get inside. Pop was smart to let Mutt and Jeffrey come over and hang out around the coop.

She sat down on a wooden bench and waited.

Once the ambulance EMTs had deferred to the coroner's office, Nick was pronounced dead. A deputy took her statement about when she'd arrived and what she'd touched.

A thought came to Christie. "Before they tow the vehicle, is there a pen in it or on Nick?"

"What?"

"A pen." She started toward the car but was held back by the deputy. "You know they always talk about people who commit suicide leaving a note, but the reality is that they rarely do. If he wrote that, then there should be a pen in the car, right?"

"Deputy, check and see if there's an ink pen in the vehicle." He turned to Christie. "Better?"

"I know it's silly, but it's just something I'd like to know."

"It's actually a good point." He pushed his thumbs into his gear belt.

"We found one." The deputy held up a pen in his latex gloved hand.

Christie knew exactly what the logo read—Webster Realty. "Hug—I mean, Sheriff Clauson...I'm sorry, still getting used to your title...do you need me for anything else?"

"No. I know where you live if I have any further questions. I do appreciate all the info given to you by Erik. I'll look into where Nick had been staying the night Kurt Matthews was killed. I spoke to Curtis again, and he says he left his gun out and the house unlocked, so it would have been easy for Nick to use his gun to kill Kurt. Then, when Curtis came back, it would look like he shot him. Only thing is, the medical examiner is reviewing his notes. The timeline for when death occurred may help to set him free. But don't get your hopes up yet. Though, with this new evidence, it may allow Curtis to get out on bail."

"Thanks, Sheriff. Now I'd like to get back to Pop before he gets worried and comes looking for me."

Kurt was gone, Curtis was in jail framed for Kurt's murder, and now, Nick was dead. Erik had now become the number one prime suspect.

Chapter Twelve

Sleep eluded Christie that night and she spent the time tossing and turning. Even after squandering the day reading the same paragraph numerous times, catching up on the many chores around the house and buying groceries, it hadn't tired her out enough to fall into a deep sleep. She finally gave up and binge-watched some shows until early in the morning. On a whim, she decided to let some fresh air into the room. She went to the window and pulled back the curtains. A flash of light caught her eye. Had Pop left the lights on in the barn? She pushed up the window, and the sound of stamping hooves and horses neighing came across the wind to her. She looked closer.

Fire!

"Fire! Pop wake up. Call the fire department!" She screamed while she shoved her feet into boots and threw on her robe over the tee-shirt and boy shorts, she'd slept in.

Pop appeared at his door, still groggy from sleep.

"Pop wake up! Call the fire department. The barn's on fire!"

She ran out to the barn, thankful that the doors had been open, and she could get the rest of the horses outside, away from the main structure. Inside, she grabbed a fire extinguisher and directed it toward the hay bale, now fully engulfed in flames. If she hadn't seen it when she did, they could have lost the entire structure, not to mention the horrible fate for the horses. Anger drove her as she fought to contain the fire.

She heard steps behind her. "Pop, I think I've—" But when she turned around, she was facing Erik.

"What are you...did you start this?" The can in her hands sputtered.

"It's all your fault. At every turn. You in the way. Now look what you've done. Nick's death is because of you." He grabbed a pitchfork and advanced toward her.

"I had nothing to do with Nick's death. If anything, you probably caused his death when you killed Kurt."

"I didn't kill Kurt. I certainly didn't kill Nick."

Christie took a step back. "Funny thing about killers. They tend to be liars, too."

"I'm not lying."

"Did Nick kill Kurt?" She searched for something to use as a weapon.

Something passed across his face. "Nick told me he'd found out that Kurt could be Curtis's son. He said he would check into it. That's all. He never said he would kill Kurt. But then he came to me and asked me to say that I'd spoken to him that evening. It all started making sense. Nick's financial problems, his constant worry about getting the property sold soon. He even said he'd been moving things around so that Curtis would start doubting his sanity and think he had dementia. I thought nothing of it at first, but then, I started putting two and two together. It had to have been Nick."

"So, you confronted him?"

Erik gripped the pitchfork tighter. "Yes. He told me everything. He'd only meant to talk to Kurt, but the guy said he was on to us. He had information that would stop everything once and for all. Nick told me it just happened. They struggled. He said it happened so quickly."

"Who else knows about this?"

"As far as I know, only Nick, me, and now, you. But I can't have you telling anyone."

Christie took a step back; the blackened hay underfoot was slippery with the foam. Soon she'd have no place to move. She had to get away from this wall. If she could just reach the door latch.

"Stop right there!" Pop's voice carried across the barn. "Back away from her. Slow and easy."

"Old man, you may have had the upper hand before, but you don't now."

Pop stepped into the barn and leveled his shotgun. "I beg to differ."

Erik broke out in laughter. "Do you think I'm so stupid as to come here knowing you had guns? You'll find that gun has no bullets in it. You may have put in a gate to the front, but it's easy to cut through Curtis's property and come in here when you're not around."

Pop responded, "How do you know I didn't add

bullets before I came in here?"

"I don't, but you shoot me, chances are you get your daughter, too." He stepped in front of Christie.

She knew that the space between them was too far for her to knock him down, plus there wasn't any way she'd win with him holding that pitchfork up in that position. Someone was bound to get hurt.

"Pop!" she yelled.

As Erik swung around toward her, he changed his hold. A loud growl sounded, and a figure jumped from the upper hayloft landing on Erik. The pair struggled, and Christie could see it was Jess. She ran toward them and pulled on the pitchfork. Erik released it, but it only gave him the ability to come up with a punch for Jess. She tossed the tool and grabbed at Erik's arm. He pushed her backward, and she fell against the open wood door of the neighboring stall. She shook her head from the impact and looked up to see something shiny. She grabbed it and went back over to the pair. Erik and Jess were fighting, fists flying. When Jess fell, Christie hurled the horseshoe at Erik. It hit him on the head and had the desired effect of knocking him out cold.

He landed with a thud into a pile of fresh manure.

"Jess, are you okay?" She ran over to the boy, who was rubbing his hands over his bloodied face. "I think so. Just don't feel so good."

"Well, you're going to have one heck of a shiner tomorrow."

He looked back at her. "Not just me. You, too."

The sound of sirens cut through the air. After the EMT's had tended to Erik, the fire department ensured that the blaze was fully out. They loaded Erik onto a gurney and strapped him down. He turned toward Christie, who was being cared for by another medical technician.

"Nick may have killed Kurt, but he didn't kill himself."

"Well, it's awfully convenient that Nick can't speak for himself about killing Kurt."

I know what you're implying." He winced and touched his hand to his head. "I'm telling you; I didn't do anything."

"You tried to burn down my barn."

"No, I didn't. It was already happening when I got

here. I'm telling you the truth."

"Sure. Like I'm going to believe anything you say."

He was loaded up into the ambulance and taken away.

"Come on guys, let's get inside." Christie ambled toward the house, while Jess, with taped bandages on his face and hand, hobbled behind.

"What were you doing in the barn hayloft?" Christie slumped down in a chair.

Jess sat across from her. "I came back earlier after being out with some friends. I planned to sleep in the trailer but saw you running out to the barn. I started around the other side to open that door, and that's when I heard you guys talking. I climbed up the outside and got into the loft that way. I thought I'd be able to figure something out from up there."

"Well, as much as I appreciate your heroics, Erik could have killed you. That pitchfork can do some damage."

"That's why I waited until he turned it sideways. The tongs were pointing down, so no one could get hurt."

Pop slapped him on the back. “Good man. That’s what makes a great man. Someone willing to do what it takes to ensure the safety of others.”

The teenager beamed at the praise.

“That’s all fine and good, but don’t do it again. I don’t want to be in a position to have to tell your dad that you’re hurt—or even worse. I already have to tell him you look like something the cat drug in.” She rose and grabbed some aspirin. “Here, this may not help much, but it’s better than nothing.” Christie swallowed two herself.

“This wouldn’t have happened if you’d been carrying, girly.”

“Pop, I already told you. I don’t want to carry a gun. Plus, I wouldn’t be sleeping with it, anyway.”

“These are scary times. If what Erik says is true, someone else set the fire in our barn.”

“Pop.” Christie ran her hand through her hair and groaned at the soreness of her raised arm. “He’s a liar. I wouldn’t believe him as far as I could throw him.”

“But what if I or Jess hadn’t been here? This could have ended a lot different.”

Christie knew Pop was right. “You know I hate guns. I don’t want one.”

“I get it. But with what’s been going on with Curtis, and now this. I don’t like knowing I may not be able to save my baby girl.”

She groaned as her muscles tightened from her earlier efforts. “I tell you what. How about I take some classes? Will that make you happy?”

“Suppose so. Now I got an appetite. How about you, Hero Man?”

Jess beamed. “Yes, sir.”

Christie refrained from saying “men.” Instead, she rose and said, “While you two eat, I’m going to take an Epsom salts bath so I can actually walk tomorrow.” She glanced at the wall clock. “Or, I guess I should say today.”

She left the pair and went into the bathroom, filling the tub with hot water and a heaping dose of the salts. Christie spied her reflection in the mirror, already a mix of green and purple covered her face where she’d hit the doorjamb. Lowering herself slowly into the heated water, she let out a deep sigh as its warmth penetrated her body.

She closed her eyes and forced herself to calm her mind, but it refused to comply. As soon as she rose from the bath, she dried off and after looking at the filthy, torn bathrobe, wrapped into a large bath towel. She heard male voices still in the kitchen as she scooted from the bathroom into her bedroom and put on clean jeans and a paisley-patterned shirt. She needed to go out and ensure the horses were okay from last night's trauma.

Her phone rang. It was Hug. "Sheriff. Good morning."

"Christie, I wanted to let you know, Erik's been discharged from the hospital. We spoke with the fire department. He couldn't have set the blaze. All we can charge him with is trespassing, but he said the gate was open to your place."

"Seriously? He attacked me."

"Technically, your dad had a gun on him. He said it was self-defense and the same when Jess jumped him."

"I can't believe this! What's going to happen?" She

towel-dried the ends of her hair.

"We have charged him with trespassing and physical assault against Jess, but that's all we can do. You can also press charges. But it wasn't enough for the judge to hold him. They let him go."

"Of course they did." She threw the towel over a chair. "Wait, does this mean Curtis can be released now?"

"Most likely. But we'll have to wait for the medical examiner to give the okay on Nick's autopsy and the note. It looks pretty cut and dry that Nick killed Kurt."

Christie sat on her bed. "That's what concerns me. It's too neat."

"Sometimes what it looks like is what it is. Let it go and move on."

She sighed. "Yep. Guess you're right. Thanks for calling." She hung up the phone when an idea occurred to her. She made her way outside to where Pop and Jess were already caring for the horses. "Pop, where are Mutt and Jeffrey?"

He whistled. No sign of the dogs. He whistled again. Nothing.

"I wondered why they didn't bark last night. Any thoughts?"

"Maybe they're over at Curtis's?"

Christie turned on her heel. "I'm going to ride over there and take a look."

Pop shouted after her. "Fine but take young Jess here with you."

She started to say there was no need, but she didn't want to fight with Pop. "All right. Come on Jess. Let's see if we can round up the boys."

She pitched Jess her keys and gingerly made her way up into the passenger side. They drove in silence to the Altgelt ranch. Coming up the drive, they saw a chicken in the mesquite tree.

"What in the—" Christie saw more of them pecking around the front yard. "I know I shut that coop the other day."

They climbed out of the truck and made their way to the coop, where two friendly, happy labs greeted them. "Ah, so that's where you are. You trust anyone, don't you?" She opened the coop and saw the remnants of a steak marrow bone. "You guys have no shame. Duped by steak?"

The labs wiggled their hindquarters, oblivious to the pretend scolding they were receiving. After Christie finagled the chickens back into the coop and watered the garden, the dogs jumped up into the truck bed, and they headed home.

They arrived to see Pop waving at them. "What is it, Pop?"

They're releasing Curtis today. They've ruled Nick's death a suicide."

"I guess that's closed then. I'm telling you, though, Curtis is getting a gate on his property, if it's the last thing I do." Christie stopped. "Wait, a minute, if it's the only thing I do."

Jess laughed. "Next thing you do."

Pop chimed in. "Most important thing you do."

"Ha. Ha. Make fun. But this I do know for sure. Curtis is getting a gate and soon. This is the last time anyone is getting onto our property. No more finding dead bodies."

Pop laughed. "Or zombies. Have you all looked in a mirror lately?"

Jess and Christie raised their arms and penguin-walked to the truck. "Feed me. Feed me," they intoned in unison.

Pop crossed his fingers in front of him. "Okay, as soon as we get Curtis. Then the chicken-fried steaks on me."

Chapter Thirteen

The weeks went by, and while the bruises healed, sleep became elusive with repeated nightmares of finding Nick and him trying to talk to her. Christie often awoke in a cold sweat. Thoughts constantly bombarded her. Finally, she went to see Orchid.

After they'd settled in with a pot of Darjeeling tea, Christie spoke. "I don't know what to do. I keep having dreams about this."

"I always believe in listening to your dreams. What do you think they mean?"

"I don't know. All I know is that I walk around Curtis's house and there's Nick's car. Why was it facing toward me? I mean if I drove there on a mission, I wouldn't have faced my car the other direction. Unless I planned on meeting someone. And I wanted to make sure I saw them when they came around the house."

Orchid sipped at her tea but said nothing.

"I've been thinking about it a lot. Maybe Nick was

meeting someone, and they killed him and made it look like suicide."

"I gather you mean his brother, Erik." Orchid made the statement matter-of-factly.

"He would have the most to gain. With Nick out of the way, that would give Erik everything that should have gone to Nick. So, it would be a win for him. Though, I never noticed any animosity between them." Christie picked up her cup.

Orchid put the cozy back over the teapot as Christie continued. "Yet, if Nick did tell him he'd killed Kurt, maybe Erik thought Nick could drag him into it. What do you think?"

"I think you never get clear answers when it comes to 'what if' questions. We know that someone killed Kurt. We don't know why and probably never will. But it makes sense that Nick met Kurt and things may have gotten out of hand. Of course, Erik could know more than he's saying but he's not going to divulge anything that implicates him. The police have stated that Nick's death was by his own hand. Who knows why he chose to park that way or even go out to Curtis's place?

Maybe he went out there with no intention of doing anything."

"But the note was Kurt's. How did he get that note?"

Orchid smiled sadly. "What-if questions again. The fact is that life is never neat and tidy. Things don't always fall into place the way you think they should. Sometimes questions remain. We must be thankful that Curtis has been released and that the charges were dropped. Also, that Erik has confessed to trespassing and assault and has paid renumeration, which will assist with any damage to the barn. Didn't you say he went back to Dallas?"

"Yes. As soon as he was allowed to leave, he hightailed it out on the first plane. I found that out from Emma."

"So, they haven't given up on buying the properties?"

"No. I think I probably made it worse by saying I had an interest. Oh, well, we'll have to deal with them. On the upside, Curtis finally agreed to the gate, and we're putting up a higher fence along the road, so hopefully, no more trespassers." She rapped on the table with her knuckles. "Knock on wood."

"That's good. You know you've had a lot happen since you came back. It's bound to take a toll on your psyche. I advise that you try to put it out of your mind. One man was killed and another one took the blame for it. Case closed."

"You're right." She sipped at her tea, but in her mind, two words haunted her: reasonable doubt. Yet, the facts were there. Erik had been arrested for the assault. Nick had been the one who had killed Kurt. It had gotten too much for him. Christie had to let it go. Nothing in this life was tidy.

Chapter Fourteen

Tears slid down Christie's cheeks as taps played at Fort Sam Houston. The Matthews had asked Christie to come when she'd stopped by to deliver a pie earlier in the week. Orchid attended the funeral with her. In head-to-toe black with a hat with a knitted black veil, Orchid looked the epitome of a traditional elderly woman.

"I'm surprised to see you dressed all in black," Christie had remarked when picking her up earlier.

"You should see all the color going on underneath this jacket. Child, I can't handle too much of this. It brings my energy down," Orchid replied.

After the service, Christie and Orchid waited to pay their respects. After they were done, Mrs. Matthews called them over. "Thank you for coming. I appreciate it, as does Lana. I've decided to return home, but she's going to stay here for a while. Thanks for helping to try and find out what happened. I'm just glad it's over now."

Christie felt Orchid clasp her wrist with a black-gloved hand. "Yes, it's over." Christie smiled at the woman, who dabbed at her eyes with a handkerchief. "I hope you'll come to the church. We're having a small reception later."

"Yes, of course. Thank you."

Inside the truck, Christie turned to Orchid. "Did you think I was going to say something?"

"Weren't you?" Orchid chided.

"Okay, yes. But you're right. What's done is done. The two people who had all the answers are gone. We...okay, *I*...have to live with that."

"Good. On another subject, how's Jess doing?"

"Much better. His heroism has been the talk of the school. But life's pretty much back to normal now."

Christie looked out at the lines of white headstones. "Yes, now it's time for the living."

Orchid nodded. "Even better."

~~~

Thank you for buying this book. You Rock!

To receive special offers, new releases, bonus content, fun giveaways, along with news about latest books or coming series,

Sign up here for my newsletter at https://www.vikkiwalton.com/

~~~

I also appreciate it when you leave a review to help determine if this book is a good read for other readers. Thanks much!

Books by Vikki Walton

Fiction

A Backyard Farming Mystery/Colorado

Chicken Culprit

Cordial Killing

Honey Homicide

A Taylor Texas Mystery

Death Takes A Break

Death Makes A Move

Death Stakes A Claim (2020)

Nonfiction Books

Work Quilting: Piece Together Diverse Income Streams, Live an Insanely Awesome Life!

The Smart Women's Guide to Travel

CPSIA information can be obtained
at www.ICGtesting.com
Printed in the USA
LVHW052342070921
697227LV00004B/168